hit the road, jack

First published in Great Britain by HarperCollins*Publishers*
77 – 85 Fulham Palace Road, Hammersmith, London W6 8JB
www.harpercollins.co.uk

1 3 5 7 9 8 6 4 2

ISBN 0 00 714278 1

Printed and bound in Great Britain by Clays Ltd, St Ives plc

hit the road, jack

mimi thebo

An imprint of HarperCollins*Publishers*

To Roger, my father

Some of us are born with our 'real' fathers and some of us get them later. I've been lucky to have had several: my own father, Roger Thebo; my stepfather, Bob Beard and my father-in-law, Tony Wadsworth. I've also had many superb teachers and mentors along the way, including Adam Smith of Oak Grove Grade School, Dan Brown of Turner High School, Professors Thurston Moore and Alan Lichter of the University of Kansas and Richard Kerridge of Bath Spa University College. If I hadn't received the guidance they all provided, I would not be writing books at all. And I am as always indebted to Andy Wadsworth, the father of my daughter Olivia, and need to thank them both for their patience and generosity.

Prologue

I had the letter in my hand. I flipped it over and I saw Dad's name signed on the other side. And then I got so excited that I couldn't read it for a moment. The blue ink just seemed to swim about on the cream coloured paper.

And I remembered...

Dad is telling me to read something. It's the same handwriting, but it's black ink on white paper. It seems to swim around in front of my eyes. I can feel his hand on my shoulder, holding on to it hard, as if he's never going to let me go. Around the page is the top of the kitchen table and I'm looking down at it. I remember that. And

I remember that the back of my head is hurting.

I'm having trouble reading it – I don't know why. Maybe it's because my head hurts. And I can hear Dad encouraging me, saying, 'Go on... read it, read it...'

Then it stopped.

I was back in the toilet with the letter in my hand. I couldn't hear Dad's voice any more. I could only hear Mum crying in her bedroom and my own breath in the small space, sounding quick and excited.

I turned the page over in my hand again. There was no date or address or anything like that. But the paper didn't feel old to me. It had that crisp feeling.

Dear Laura,

I'm working hard, but I miss you so much. I just don't like being apart.

It gets really cold here, and the food is terrible. But the worst part is being all alone.

I know what we planned and I know it would be better for us if I stayed here and kept on at it, but I just don't think I can.
I'll try and speak to you this weekend. Maybe I can make you understand and you'll let me come home.
You are my only darling Laura,
John

It was so sad it made me feel sick. My dad was out there somewhere, working hard. He only wanted to come home. But instead, my mother was going to marry Richard.

She thought I was asleep. That was the only reason she even got these letters out. She'd always told me that my dad had never written to us or called us. But that was obviously a lie. My dad wrote to us all the time. He wanted to come home and she wouldn't let him. No wonder it made her cry to read the letters. At least I knew she wasn't *all* bad. At least lying and cheating and being mean hurt her enough to make her cry.

I turned off the toilet light and opened the door very slowly. I looked in her door again – she was still lying on her stomach, crying. The letters were all over the bed and some of them had fallen on the floor. There were dozens of them. All from my father. All begging to come home, I bet. I threw the one in my hand inside the door and went back to my room.

I wasn't all that quiet, either. I didn't even care if she caught me. But she didn't. She just kept crying. I could hear her even when I got into bed.

I lay there and played my new memory over and over again in my head. My dad. Squeezing my shoulder. Encouraging me. 'Go on!' he'd said. 'Go on!' Somewhere, he was out there in the night. All alone.

1.

Hit the Road, Jack

It had been six days since I'd read the letter and I hadn't spoken a single word to my mother the whole time.

It was starting to bother her. I could tell by the way she put my spaghetti down in front of me – too gently, as if she was trying really hard not to slam it on the table. I could tell because she had the little line between her eyes. She only gets that little line when she's desperately worried about something.

I hadn't seen that line stay for so long in five years... since she threw my dad out of the house. I was glad to see it there. It meant I was winning.

Success always gives me an appetite. I took a huge roll of pasta on my fork and shoved it into my mouth, letting the sauce dribble down my chin.

'Jack!' she scolded me.

For an answer, I opened my mouth and showed her my half-chewed bite.

She jumped up quickly and went to the sink, but I could tell she was upset. Then, for the one hundred and twenty eighth time in those six days, she tried to talk to me. She came and sat down, wiping her face with the tea towel.

She said, 'I'm not marrying Richard to get at you, Jack.' Her voice sounded tired. 'I'm marrying Richard because he makes me happy. I deserve to be happy.'

I came really close to losing the game right then. I wanted to speak to her. I wanted to tell her she didn't deserve *anything*. I wanted to tell her I knew all about Dad's letters and that she was a cold-hearted cow.

The only way I could shut myself up was to take another big bite of pasta.

I let the sauce drool down over my chin again, while I stared right into her worried eyes.

Her face collapsed in on itself and she ran up the stairs to her bedroom. I was left with only a steaming plate of spaghetti across from me, getting cold on the table.

I could hear her start to cry. I could hear her pick up the telephone.

You can hear almost everything in our house from the kitchen, if it's quiet enough. Sitting there all alone, it was definitely quiet enough.

Oh, yeah, I was winning the game, all right. But I wasn't hungry any more.

I was just sitting there, staring at my plate, when Richard arrived. He came in the back door. Nobody uses their front door in my street, unless it's for someone like the police or the census people.

Richard walked through the kitchen at about a million miles an hour and didn't even slow down when he tossed his jacket on my mum's chair. He pointed at me and said, 'Don't move.' And then he ran up the stairs, too.

I could hear Mum and Richard talking, even hear him say something about 'telling him'. I could hear my mum wail the word 'no'.

They were quiet for a moment. I knew 'him' had to be me. Had they been talking about the letters? Or some *other* secret? The voices started up again and then I could hear them walking around. Somebody used the phone, then it got quiet. Finally, I heard Richard coming back down the stairs.

He said, 'Your grandparents are coming over. Let's get this place cleared up.'

I scraped all the spaghetti into the bin. Shame really, it was my favourite. Then I filled a bowl with soapy water and did the washing-up. Richard hoovered in the living room, coming through sometimes with things for the bin. At last he emptied that and put in a new liner. I was just letting the water out when he came to wash his hands at the sink and then looked for the tea towel.

My mum had run upstairs with it. He had to get a new one out of the drawer. And then he had to get another one out to dry the dishes while I wiped down the surfaces. He hadn't said much.

I sat back down at the table and watched him while he got a tea tray together. He knew where everything was, of course. He'd been spending weekends at my house for nearly two years.

I watched him flick his fringe out of his eyes as he sorted through the biscuit tin, watched how his bony elbows were working through his new jumper, just like they'd done on his old one.

I mean, Richard was OK. I had nothing against Richard.

But when the tea tray was done and he had to turn around, I could see in his eyes he definitely had something against me. He said, 'I don't know how you can stand acting like this, Jack.'

I didn't know either. Being horrible didn't come all that naturally to me and I felt a bit sick about it. I opened my mouth to say something, but I didn't know what to say. Richard waited. And then I shut it again. I shrugged instead.

Richard shook his head. He said, 'Oh, Jack.' And then he said, 'Go and change your shirt.'

Upstairs, I avoided looking at myself in the mirror. The spaghetti sauce had run all over my collar. I'd never done that before, let sauce run down my face. Some kids do it at school every day. How do they keep the sauce off their collars?

I went into the bathroom and washed my face and neck with my flannel, half turned away from the sink, still avoiding my reflection. I listened, but I couldn't hear anything from my mother's room. Then I put on a fresh top. It smelled nice.

Just as I reached the bottom of the stairs, there was a knock on the door and my grandparents came in.

I was really surprised.

I thought it would be Poppa and Nana Lacey – my mum's parents. But it wasn't. It was my dad's parents, Poppa and Nana Burke. I hadn't seen them for months.

It felt really good to be hugged. Poppa and Nana Burke were glad to see me. Right then, it seemed like they were the only people in the world who were actually happy that I existed.

We went into the sitting room. They took the

sofa and Richard took the chair. I hunched on to the footstool. Suddenly, I was ravenous again. I wanted a biscuit but when I took a chocolate digestive, everyone looked at me. I felt silly holding it, so I stuffed the whole thing in my mouth at once. I almost choked trying to chew it all with my mouth shut.

'Where's Laura?' Nana Burke asked. Poppa Burke just dealt with his cup of tea. His hands were really shaky. Every time I saw him, he looked worse. It was his liver. It was worn out and there was nothing much they could do. He was too old to get another one. I remembered when he was really big and kind of scary-looking. But now he was all bent over and pale.

Richard answered Nana Burke. 'Upstairs,' he said. 'I made her get some rest. She's really in no shape to talk right now.'

Nana Burke sighed. She looked at me and said, 'Oh, Jonathan,' in this way she has. She starts off high and ends up low. It sounds like she's letting her voice fall down a well.

Her and Poppa were the only people on earth

who called me Jonathan. Mum always says that Nana Burke has had a load of troubles in her time. Right then she looked as if she had. If I'd felt a bit horrible before, I felt really terrible then, just for making her have one more.

I could feel biscuit crumbs on my fingers. I dusted off my hands so that I didn't have to look at her any more.

Nana Burke sighed again when Richard said, 'So. I thought it might help if you could talk to Jack about his father.'

Poppa Burke snorted and, if you closed your eyes, sounded big and scary again. 'Waste of space,' he grunted.

'James!' Nana Burke sounded shocked.

'Got to be said.' Poppa's eyes were glaring, sunk into his yellow old face. 'Your father,' he said, 'hasn't written or called or bog all for five years.' He was getting worked up, which wasn't good for him, and little bits of spit were flying out of his mouth. 'His mum goes into hospital – nothing. His sister dies, *dies*. Nothing. Not a card to his mother, not a tenner for the little kiddies she left behind. Not even flowers.'

He stopped to gasp for air and we all looked at him with our mouths hanging open. I don't think I'd ever heard him say so much before in my whole life. 'You want some advice, sonny?' he asked me, and then repeated himself, barking the words at me. 'You want some advice?'

I nodded rapidly. The tone in his voice was powerful. Nodding didn't seem enough. It felt like I should jump to attention and salute or something.

'Forget him.'

Poppa Burke kind of deflated after this and sank into the cushions on the sofa. One by one, we all shut our mouths. He wasn't scary any more.

Nana Burke said, 'Well,' in an aggrieved and disturbed voice, as if someone had done something unpleasant, like farted or spilled tea on the carpet. She angled her knees towards where I was sitting on the floor and said, 'Jonathan, your father loves you. I know he does. I saw his face the day you were born.' Nana Burke has really pretty eyes, sparkly green eyes.

When you look into Nana Burke's eyes, it almost takes your mind off the way her jaw doesn't fit her quite right and the lopsided look of her face in general.

Mum says she was pretty, really pretty, a long time ago. She won't tell me what happened to make Nana Burke's face not fit together any more.

Nana Burke sighed again. 'But your father has lots of problems. I'm sure he *wanted* to come to the hospital *and* to Mary's funeral. I'm sure he *wants* to come and see you. But he's...'

'Ha!' Poppa Burke barked. And then he coughed again, this time for a long, long time. So long that Nana Burke had to rummage in her handbag for something and Richard ran into the kitchen for a glass of water. And then Richard was helping Poppa stand up again and then he walked them to the car and then they were gone.

It felt like we were almost talking about something real for a moment. But then it was over so fast.

Would I have talked to them about the letters if they'd been able to stay? I don't know.

I know I wouldn't have talked to Richard.

Because when Richard and I were alone and cleaning up the tea things and he said, 'Look, are you going to give your mum a break?' all I could do was mumble.

'Sorry.' That was all I said.

Should I have said something to Richard? Probably. I mean, of course. Of course, I should have talked to Richard about the letter, about the whole thing. It certainly would have saved everyone a lot of trouble if I had.

I was almost thirteen, too old to think what I thought, maybe.

I thought my dad could solve everything. I thought Dad could make everything all right.

I just had to find him.

2.

Still is the Night

I suppose for some kids my age, leaving the house after dark would be no big deal. But it was for me. I mean, it was a school night and I was on my own. I didn't tell anyone where I was going or what I was doing or when I'd be back. I'd never done anything like it before.

I'm not sure I really want to write down just how sad and geeky I am. But I'll write this – I'd never knowingly broken a rule before in my entire life.

So me leaving the house was pretty mega.

I zipped up my jacket as I walked down the close to the main road of our estate. It was getting cold. Bonfire night had been two weeks ago and Christmas was ahead. Some people on the estate already had their Christmas lights on. Some people even had a tree in the window.

There's no real reason to tell you about the estate or the close or the road that leads into town. There's no real reason even to tell you all that much about the town. It's just a town. It tried to be a city last year but it lost out to Brighton.

Typical.

It's that kind of place, not really one thing and not really the other. It's even pretty much right in the middle of the country. Let's just call it Nowhere.

Nowhere isn't known for its architecture or design, if you know what I mean. There's no stately homes to look at or tree-lined avenues to enjoy. There's no fountains or sculptures or anything like that. There's just loads of houses like ours – put up in about twenty minutes as cheaply as possible sometime in the eighties – with little parades of shops thrown in every so often. A dry-cleaners, a takeaway, a newsagent's and maybe a pub. Enough to let people survive. But not exactly live.

It was boring. And so I replayed my new memory in my head, trying to work it into the other ones I had.

There's not very many of them.

I can remember my mum and dad dancing together in front of a Christmas tree. I think that's the first one because I must have been really tiny. In it, I see their knees more than anything else. But sometimes I must look up because I see my mother smiling, happier than I think I've ever seen her since.

I can remember going to a football match. That one gets a bit scary, if I'm honest. Dad was shouting and screaming and the veins on his neck were standing out. I was a bit worried my dad was mental or something before I watched a World Cup game with Dill and his father. Now I think football just makes some people get like that.

And then another one of Mum and Dad dancing. It's different from the Christmas one. I can't see my mother's face and I can't hear any music. I can just remember the sound of their feet. I think they must be in the kitchen, their feet are too loud to be on carpet.

And now the one with the letter, or whatever it was in my dad's handwriting, and him encouraging me to read it.

That was it. That was everything I knew about my father. Except...

I knew my dad was homeless.

I was only about eight when I heard someone tell my mother that they'd seen my father 'sleeping rough on the street'. That same year, somebody in my old school heard about it. And I thought I'd never hear the end of it.

My old school wasn't great. I didn't have a lot of friends there – for all kinds of reasons. They didn't pick on me just because my dad was homeless. It only gave them *another* reason. But I think I've heard every bad name homeless people can be called, because I got called them all, that whole year.

They all came into my mind as I took that long, lonely walk. *Bum, Crusty, Beggar, Gyppo, Loser...*

I was walking faster and faster, as if I could outrun the memories. The time they cornered me in the toilets. The time they caught me walking home.

My legs were pumping. Downtown Nowhere is actually down. Downhill, I mean. I'd been going too fast when it got steep and now to stop myself from falling forward I had to nearly run. The muscles around my knees felt weak and shaky and my shins were hurting. Bam, bam, bam – my trainers had lost a lot of their traction and were slapping against the pavement. Every slap had a little slide hidden inside it. I wasn't in control of my feet at all. I was sure I was going to fall.

And then it levelled out a bit. I stopped and leaned my hands on my knees to catch my breath.

That's sad enough, isn't it? Being that weak? But what made it even worse was that I could have taken a bus – I could have taken a *taxi* if I'd wanted to. I had over seventy pounds at home, hidden in my sock drawer. I'd been saving it up all year to get my mum a really nice Christmas present.

But I was such a hopelessly geeky saddo that even though I hated my mum, I never even *considered* using that money. So I nearly killed myself walking into town, instead.

Suddenly, it occurred to me – how was I going to make it back? The hill was a monster. I'd die if I had to walk it. But it looked like I wasn't going to have a choice. I only had about twenty pence in my pocket.

The only thing that made me feel any better was thinking about how worried my mum would be when she found out I was gone. She was going to go crazy. As I started to walk again, past the older, posher houses on the wider streets near the centre, that thought made me smile. In spite of everything.

I don't know what I thought I would find when I finally got to downtown Nowhere. People lined up neatly in sleeping bags, I suppose. Alphabetical order or something. I'd just skip the As, go down the Bs and there my dad would be, sitting up in a sleeping bag, waiting for me.

Of course, it wasn't like that.

It wasn't even eleven o'clock. The pubs were still open. Burger King was still open. Even the Tesco Metro was still open. And the people were all upright and walking around.

When I passed Burger King, you could smell the fries from their heat exhaust. Again, I thought of that seventy pounds and how I hadn't eaten my dinner. I mean, burger chain fast food isn't the best thing in the world for you, but it does have *some* nutritional value. It's better than nothing. And did you know you could save yourself 68% of the fat content if you don't have cheese or go large?

The milkshakes, too, have a surprisingly good protein and energy to fat ratio. They also have over 150 ingredients, most of which are binders, preservatives, flavour enhancers and antioxidants. But they're cheap and keep you alive. Besides, I really love a thick chocolate milkshake, even though I know what makes them so thick and creamy didn't come out of a cow.

I was hungry, really hungry, after my walk. And I was going to stay hungry. I was also going to get even more tired, climbing that hill to get home instead of sitting in a nice, warm taxi.

I remember sighing before I thought about the task at hand. My dad was there. Somewhere.

There were quite a lot of people out, for a weekday night. How could you tell which ones were sleeping on the streets when they weren't sleeping?

I wandered around the pedestrianised section looking at all the men's faces. I always looked at men's faces. I was always looking for my dad. Only this time I wasn't with anybody else. I didn't have to hide what I was doing. Or that's what I thought, anyway.

'What are you looking at?' Some huge bellied man in a Chelsea strip bellowed in my face.

I couldn't say anything. He was enormous. His shiny shirt stretched over an incredible expanse of fat. His face was big and red and about five inches away from mine.

'Well?' he shouted and I could smell the beer on his breath. Then he and his friends started to laugh. One of them said something about 'wetting himself' and I knew he meant me. I went red, and they staggered off, laughing.

I licked my lips and tried to get my heart to slow back down.

What was it about me that made people want to torture me? What did I do wrong? Was it the way I looked? My hair or something? I stood there, wondering if my whole life was going to be like this, if anyone who wanted was just going to be able to come up and mess with me, over and over, until the day I died.

'All right?'

And here was someone else, someone new to try and hurt me. This time it was another kid, about my age, maybe a little older.

The kids, in my experience, were always a lot worse. Again, my voice refused to work. I just nodded at him, trying bravely to make eye contact, to put on some show of not being scared to death. I didn't manage the eyes, I just focused on his sharp chin. He was short, but he seemed to be older than me.

'New?'

I cleared my throat and managed to ask, 'What do you mean?'

'I an't seen you around.'

Another kid circled in from my left. He had the same sharp, foxy kind of face. They were both wearing puffa jackets, with short haircuts and new-looking trainers. The second boy was even shorter than the first one. I thought he was older, too. It was like they aged the wrong way, shrinking instead of growing.

They never stopped moving, considering me from all angles. I just stood there, wishing they'd go away.

'I an't seen him, either.'

'Must be new. Are you new?'

I shrugged. 'I s'pose so,' I said. 'I haven't been down here before... I mean, not on my own.'

'On your own, are you?'

I shouldn't have said that, I realised. I shrugged again, trying to look unconcerned.

'What's your name?' the first one asked.

I didn't want to tell him.

'What's your name?' he asked again.

'Are you deaf?' the second one asked.

There was a hissing sound and both boys looked up. It was a girl, just at the edge of one of the alleyways. She said, 'Leave him. Countess wants you two. Job on.' Suddenly, the boys weren't there anymore. I looked around and I couldn't see them walking away in any direction. It was like they'd melted into the night air.

'S'not nice, is it?' The girl had spoken again. 'S'not nice, being on your own.'

'Daisy!' a voice called. It was a grown up voice, male and rough. The girl gave me a little smile which I could hardly see and then I could hardly see *her*. And then I couldn't.

The whole thing was really spooky.

I was sweating again and my legs felt weak. There was a bench a few metres away and I collapsed on to it, as if I'd just run a marathon or something.

'*Big Issue*? Would you like to buy a *Big Issue*, madam? *Big Issue*?'

In the middle of the cobbled street a vendor was working. He was working hard, selling like anything, bowing and waving his magazine at people. Sometimes somebody bought one. He wore boots and jeans and a couple of jumpers, a bigger one over a smaller one, and fingerless gloves. He also had this mad hat with earflaps. And a dog. A rottweiler. All curled up at his feet on what seemed to be half a blanket.

People who sold the *Big Issue* were homeless. I thought it made sense to ask one homeless person about another homeless person. He might even know my dad.

So, as soon as I could get my legs to work, I walked over to him and waited until the crowd from the cinema had all passed by.

I said, 'Excuse me. I think you might be able to help me. I'm look—'

He was busy putting money away inside the waist of his jeans and wouldn't even look up. He interrupted me, saying, 'Mate, I can hardly help myself. Go to Social Services if you can't hack the street.'

Why did everyone think I was homeless? I looked down at my old coat, the baggy jumper Nana Burke had knitted me last Christmas, my faded blue jeans and dirty old supermarket trainers. I reckon Mum didn't spend a lot of money on my after-school clothes. I'd never really noticed before.

'I'm not homeless,' I said.

'Then go home.' He was counting the magazines left in his bag.

'I'm looking for my dad.'

He lost count, swore, and started again. 'Go to the police, if you're lost. Just *leave me alone*!' The rottweiler looked up at me with a very serious expression. A small but intimidating rumble started in the back of its throat.

I started to go but something made me turn back. 'It's not me that's lost. It's my dad. He's the one who's on the street.'

The vendor looked at me for the first time, really looked at me. And I didn't have any trouble meeting his eyes. They were brown and as they looked at me, they seemed to soften.

'Oh,' he said and pushed his cap back off his forehead. 'That's a different kettle of fish, then, isn't it?'

The rottweiler whined and half sat up. The vendor laughed. 'No, Tarka. Not fish supper. Not tonight.'

She flopped back down and curled back up. Her big brown eyes looked sorrowful.

'Stroke her if you want. She won't hurt you.'

The dog's coat was smooth and warm. I stroked her head and she closed her eyes, enjoying it.

The vendor looked around and then began to gather up his stuff and put it in his bag. 'I think that's me done for tonight,' he said. 'Not a bad day, as days go.'

Tarka slowly cleaned my hand with her tongue.

'Have you got a picture? A picture of your dad?'

I stood up and wiped my drooly hand on the seat of my jeans. 'No.'

'Can you get one?'

I thought about it. 'Yeah, probably.'

He smiled at me. He had a nice smile, though he was missing a couple of bottom teeth. His face had that same not-quite-fitting-together look as Nana Burke. He said, 'I'm here most nights. Get a bunch of photocopies and come back. I might be able to help you.'

Come back? Mum was never going to let me out of her sight again. Not after this. I had to do it tonight!

I said something of this to the vendor, but he just smiled. 'Oh,' he said, 'Getting out of the house isn't ever much of a problem. It's the getting back in again that's the trick.'

I watched him snap on Tarka's lead. 'What's your name?' he asked me.

I told him. He said, 'I'm Andy.' He stuck out his hand and I shook it.

But it wasn't until he was almost around the corner that I shouted, 'Thank you!'

He didn't turn around, but he waved his free hand above his head.

Once he was gone, the shadows from the alleys seemed to seep into the square. I looked around, trying to see if anything was moving in them. My back twitched under my coat, as if a hundred eyes were watching me.

I walked as fast as I could out of town towards my estate. I had to stop more than once. My thighs burned with lactic acid and my lungs ached trying to pump enough oxygen into my blood to shift it. I hurt so badly that the second time I stopped, tears flooded my eyes. The street seemed to stand straight up, like a wall. I had to force myself to take another step.

With every agonising step, I dreaded what it would be like when I finally got home. I imagined Mum and Richard would shout at me until my ears bled, until my whole head deflated like a punctured balloon. There would be lights blazing and a police car outside and half the neighbourhood out looking for me with torches. I'd be locked in my room on bread and water for the next fortnight and Andy and Tarka would forget all about me.

It felt hopeless, hurting this much to get to a place where there was going to be a horrible scene.

But there wasn't a *horrible* scene. There wasn't any scene at all.

The house was dark. The kitchen door was locked, but I took my emergency key out of my wallet and opened it ever so quietly. Richard's car was still in the drive, but there were no sounds of talking or of anything else. As quietly as I could, I remembered to lock the door behind me.

I took off my shoes like they do in the movies and crept up the stairs. I didn't even switch on my light but put my pyjamas on by touch. The house was so quiet that I jumped when the refrigerator came on down in the kitchen. For a second it sounded like the house was falling down.

I slid under the duvet and it felt funny. I felt dirty without a wash and my teeth felt all furry and disgusting. I thought to myself, I'll never be able to get to sleep like this.

3.

Ain't nothin' like the real thing

I just wrote a whole chapter and then deleted the entire thing. It was a great chapter, all about how I walked to school the next day with Dad's picture in my rock-climbing backpack, and how I defeated the school bully with my bravery and cunning and how my girlfriend worshipped me and how I was really good at football.

The only problem was it was all lies.

I reckon there's going to be no way to hide my total geekiness. I might as well just write in big letters ULTRA SAD WEEDY GEEKOID DWEEB and get it over with.

Because the thing about a story like this one is that if you don't tell the truth, it's just not worth *anything*. I mean, if you don't tell the truth, you might as well put a really nice dad back in the house and make it a really posh house and *everything*. And then there's no reason to write it down at all. Because it won't do me any good.

So. The truth.

Richard drove me to school. He does this nearly every morning, even when he hasn't spent the night at our house. It's a little out of his way, but he doesn't really mind because (and this is the worst bit) *he's a teacher at my school*.

I didn't get threatened by the school bully because there isn't one. I go to this special school for gifted girls and boys. It's an academic centre of excellence where we're *all* pretty much sad geeks. I mean, some of us aren't freaks of nature. Some of the girls are pretty and some of the boys are good at sports. But they're the minority. The rest of us wear glasses, or look like we should, and get excited about logarithmic tables and computer languages. Up until the night I saw my mum reading my dad's letters, all I could think about was the science project I'm working on for the town science competition. I'm doing it with Dill Hanson and it's about frog nutrition. We get extra merit marks, but actually we're doing it *for fun*.

I know. I'm sorry. And if you want to close this book right now, I'll completely understand.

I don't have a girlfriend. I do have a girl that hangs out in my group. Her name is Anne. The boys are Scott, Dill and Wesley. And they look just like they sound. The only one a tiny bit interesting is Scott. He's got cerebral palsy, so at least he has an excuse for being weedy. And he works really hard to walk and do the things that we all do without thinking about it. So he gets some credit for being brave. The rest of us are so sad that we've all admitted sometimes we're jealous of him for that.

And as for football, I don't know anything about it. That one memory of my dad acting a bit mental must have put me off.

So. If you're still there, I'll continue. Only this time with the truth.

That morning, I opened my mum's wardrobe while she was in the shower. Richard had gone home to shower and change, so I had five clear minutes to get the shoebox down where mum kept the photos and select one of dad. I got the most recent one I could find, one of the ones after he'd started getting a little fat. I've noticed that once people start getting fat they usually keep going. I think it's something to do with... but I won't bore you with that.

Breakfast was a bit weird, to tell you the truth. It was OK when it was just me not talking to Mum. But now Mum wasn't talking to me. She looked pale but calm as she gave me some Marmite toast and a glass of grapefruit juice. She knows I hate Marmite *and* grapefruit. I thought I saw her smile as I dumped the toast in the bin and poured the juice down the sink. I noticed that the line between her eyes was gone.

My breakfast was an apple that I ate in the car.

Richard was still talking to me. But not about anything important. It was like they'd given up... but I knew my mum better than that.

I had the picture in my satchel and managed to scan it into the computer during lab. Then I did this killer poster and printed out twenty-five of them. I don't think anybody even noticed. I was supposed to be doing internet research and you're always printing stuff off when you're doing that. If I'd done colour, though, someone would have noticed all right. The lab colour printer is really slow and noisy. So I did them all in black and white.

That didn't really matter because Dad and I have the same colouring. That light, mousey hair they call dishwater blond, pale blue eyes and pale skin with cheeks that get red all too easily.

In colour Dad looked OK. But when I saw the black and white ones, his eyes looked really small and piggy. And his face looked puffy.

I asked Dill to do me a favour and he did the frog weigh-in and strength measurements on his own that day. I used that time to do my homework. Or kind of *half* do some of it. Not as well as I usually do, but well enough so that none of my teachers would think I hadn't done it at all.

I didn't need anyone discussing my performance with Richard.

I was starving by lunchtime. I ate my entire plateful, even though it was horrid soupy lasagne.

Everyone kind of talked around me and over me. I couldn't concentrate on what they were saying. And then I remembered...

I'm hungry, really hungry, just like I am now. I'm cold, as well, and my bottom feels wet. My mum is handing me a plate and we're in the kitchen, but we're not at the table, we're pressed into a corner under a pile of clothes that smell bad. Washing. We're sitting under a pile of washing.

My hand is shaking as I reach for the plate. There's only some frozen peas on it.

'Put them in your mouth, a few at a time,' my mum says. Her hair is lank and greasy and her face is shiny. One side is shinier than the other, it looks puffy. Her breath smells bad. 'When they get warm, you can chew them.'

She is whispering and I know I mustn't make a sound. The peas are hard and cold in my mouth...

'What do you think, Jack? Jack?' Anne was saying my name and it pulled me back into the cafeteria. I still couldn't say anything: my mind felt like it was uploading data or something, it was busy; it couldn't take any time for me now.

I heard Dill say, 'I told you, he's completely spaced out.'

I finally managed to say, 'I am not,' even though it was a lie. 'I'm just hungry.'

'What?' Anne said, 'For that?' She pointed to her untouched lasagne. 'You can have mine if you want.'

'And mine,' Wesley said.

They sat in horrified silence as I scoffed the lot.

'Wha-what is *with* you?' Scott asked me. I just shrugged.

I could see Anne's eyes meet Dill's. I knew they'd talk about me later.

However much I might fool my teachers that things were normal, I wasn't going to be able to fool that crowd for long. Like I said, we're all pretty clever.

But I wasn't ready to talk about it yet. Leaving the house... meeting Andy and Tarka... it seemed like a dream sitting at those long, yellow tables in the cafeteria at school.

It seemed even less real than the odd memory. Frozen peas? Dirty washing? What was that all about?

I blinked, looking around the big room, the sunlight leaking through the ceiling, the sound of talking and eating bouncing off the white tiled walls.

Nothing in my mind seemed real when I looked around that room. And how can you talk about something if it isn't even real?

4.

Soul Man

After the dinner my mum made me – a Brussels sprout soufflé with garlic and olive oil mashed potatoes and a warm spinach salad – and after the way she and Richard ate all theirs with relish and smirked at me trying to pick my way around the less gross bits of the soufflé and potatoes to try and find *something* I could actually eat... After *that*, you'd think I'd be more than willing to spend some of her Christmas money on a bus into town. And maybe a burger at Burger King.

But no.

Loser that I am, I walked it again.

I did, however, think to make myself a sandwich

before I left the house. It was a little later than it had been the night before. Richard had gone home with his marking and Mum was watching the television she keeps in her room – the one she usually just uses to watch her soap operas when there's something good that I want to watch on the main telly. The coast was clear for me to sneak out and to make myself something to eat.

But they'd thought of that. There wasn't any soft cheese or peanut butter or anything I liked in any of the cupboards or the fridge. There was only French stick bread, Marmite, some sort of mushroom pâté that looked grim as death, and a wedge of cheese that smelled like it had passed its sell-by date some time in the Pleistocene era. I checked the freezer. No oven chips. No burgers. No fish fingers. Back to the cupboards. None of the cereals I liked, only Grape Nuts and muesli. And anyway, she'd bought skimmed milk. Even the jam was extra-tart lime marmalade.

And the biscuit barrel was empty.

So I crept out of the kitchen door and locked it behind me with nothing to eat but a hunk of

French stick with butter. It would keep me alive, but it wasn't ideal. Where was the protein? Where was the taste, for that matter?

I had Dad's posters in a carrier bag. At first this felt light enough, but by the time I was halfway there, it seemed like I had bricks in the bottom of the thing.

It was another clear, frosty night. I'd worn my walking boots. Richard had bought me them for Scouts. I hated Scouts.

Anyway, with my big boots I didn't slip around as much, which helped on the way downtown. Even though my muscles were still sore from the night before, my legs didn't feel quite as shaky. I started off feeling cold, but I was able to move pretty fast down the hill. By the time I got to the pedestrianised section of downtown, I had my jacket unzipped and was sweating a little under my jumper.

I was going at a good rate. So good that I nearly fell over when someone grabbed my collar.

'You're the new boy.'

It was a female voice. The pressure on my collar

relaxed and I turned to see the girl from the night before. The first thing I thought was 'anorexia'. I mean, she was so thin that I was surprised she could even walk, let alone grab me that hard. Especially in those high shoes she was wearing.

She looked me up and down, her eyes narrowing. 'I remember you,' she said. 'How you're all alone.' She kind of sang the last two words, 'all aloooone,' and made a little sad face. 'It's not nice to be all alone, is it?'

It was silly to be scared of this girl. She looked older than me, but she was still a kid. And even I could have broken her in half like a stick. Still, my heart started to pound in my ears.

Her twiggy fingers pushed into my hair, fluffing it. 'I think you need some friends,' she said softly.

I pulled my head away. 'I have friends,' I said. At least I think I do, I thought. Unless... unless they're just really nice kids who feel a bit sorry for me. Because suddenly I wondered if Anne, Dill, Scott and Wesley really *were* my friends, or if they were only acting like it. The girl had the kind of voice that makes you wonder things like that.

'And where are they now? Hmm?' She leaned her head to one side. Her hair was all caught up in a ponytail on top of it. Her eyes looked enormous and they had make-up around them, really thick. 'Where are your friends now? Why did they leave you all alone?'

Because I didn't tell them anything about this, I thought to myself. Or maybe, I didn't tell them because they'd leave me all alone *anyway*. I tried to remember the cafeteria. How sunny it had been, how Anne had looked at Dill, worried about me. But it seemed like a dream, here, with the carrier bags and newspapers littering the pavement, and the kids all sick and hard. And me, alone.

She reached out with one of her long, knobbly fingers and stroked the side of my face. Her finger was as cold as glass and she smelled musty, like a wet book.

'Poor boy. I think I should take you to meet my best friend. Would you like to meet the Countess?' Her eyes rolled towards mine. I couldn't swallow. I felt like I couldn't breathe. And then she looked down.

'Ooooh!' she cooed. 'Someone has new shoes! Now, how did a lonely little boy get nice new shoes?'

I mumbled. 'Richard gave me them.'

'Did he? He must like you.'

I wished I hadn't said anything. Her big eyes narrowed and she moved back a little. 'And what did you do for *Richard*?' She said Richard's name in a horrible way. I wished even harder that I hadn't said anything.

I thought of Andy waiting for me. He popped into my mind like a picture, with Tarka standing by his side. I said, 'I've got to go,' to myself and then louder, to her. Then I managed to stumble one step away.

That one step was all it took to break the spell. I started to run. Nobody stopped me.

Andy smiled at me. 'So,' he said, 'You managed to get out of the house.'

I was a little puffed from my sprint, so I just took out one of the posters and handed it to him. He sucked his teeth. 'He looks a little familiar,' he said. 'But not that familiar. I'm sure I've seen him around sometime, though. I just can't remember where.'

Everything I'd done that day, all that I'd gone through, and Andy couldn't even help me. It was all I could do not to start blubbing like a baby. Even Tarka sat up, as if she could feel something was wrong. I turned to start the long climb back home.

'Hey, Jack,' Andy had grabbed my arm. 'Don't worry, mate. There's loads of other people we can ask.' He looked around at the dwindling crowd. 'I'll just pack up here and we'll start.'

And what was odd was that I came even closer to crying then, when he *was* helping me. My voice croaked when I thanked him.

He just smiled his crooked smile again.

While he put his money in his jeans and buttoned his top jumper, I folded Tarka's blanket and snapped her lead on. Then he bundled all of his stuff into and on top of his bag and we set off.

'Where do *you* sleep, Andy?'

'I'm cool now,' he said. 'I finally found a B&B

that would take Tarka. And I'm in line for a flat. Should be next month.'

'But you still sell the *Big Issue*?'

He shrugged. 'I'm working on that, too. I'm doing this computer course and learning to read and write a bit better than I can right now. My vocational officer says that with my customer skills, I'd be a natural for a call centre job. Maybe by Easter, he says.'

I was quiet for a moment. It just didn't seem like anyone should have to work that hard to get a call centre job. And then I said, with as much enthusiasm as I could, 'That's really great, Andy.'

He must have seen through me, because he said, 'No. It's not really great. It's just really normal. And that's all I need to be these days. Just normal. Maybe later I can work on being great.'

It made me a bit ashamed of myself, to be honest. I wasn't even thirteen yet, but I knew I would probably make scads of money. Anne and the other kids I hung out with at school were already thinking about setting up a company together, to develop new foods. They wanted me in R&D – Research and Development.

Even if that didn't work out, I could work for someone else. And even if I chose to do pure research, at some university or something, I'd still make a good wage – good enough, anyway. I didn't know what to say, so I asked, 'Where are we going?'

'To see Otis. He knows everybody.'

There's this big posh pub just off the pedestrianised section of Nowhere. It's a pub, but it looks more like a restaurant. They have really excellent food there. It's Richard and Mum's favourite place and they have to save up to go there. They took me once, at lunchtime. The pudding came in a huge bowl just swimming in real vanilla custard. It was the most fantastic thing I'd ever tasted.

Andy and Tarka and I looked more than a bit out of place. The customers coming out of the big yellow squares of light were all in nice designer gear and they walked around us like we were a puddle.

Andy didn't seem to even notice. He said, 'There he is.'

There was an old black man with his head down, fiddling with a karaoke machine. Suddenly, trumpets burst out of the surprisingly small speaker and he stood up and started to kind of wiggle in place to the music. He had a woolly jumper on, but over it he wore a pinstriped suit. He had a pork-pie hat and dark glasses. And he had thin, elegant shoes. He was sliding over the pavement like it was polished oak or something.

And then he started to sing. 'You didn't have to do what you did, but you did, yes you did – and I THANK YOU.' If I'd been surprised that such a big sound could come out of the little karaoke machine, I was pretty well blown away by Otis's voice. It was incredible. Really, really good.

People just stopped in their tracks to listen. At the end of the song, they threw money in the velvet-lined box at his feet. Pound coins, mostly. But some didn't leave. They were waiting for the next tune.

'One more,' Andy said, 'and then we'll ask him.'

I had never even heard music like Otis sang. The next one was amazing. 'THINK!' Otis shouted,

'You'd better think about, what you're trying to do to me!' His voice climbed up and down, got quiet and then got loud again. Usually, I'm hopeless at feeling rhythm – I'm a really bad dancer. But this I could feel. I think because the words and the music went together so closely. I could barely stand still.

The posh people were clapping their hands. When Otis stopped, a lot of them cheered. Then they threw a lot more money in his box and started to drift away. Otis felt his way to sit on a little folding stool and wiped his face with a big silk handkerchief he took out of his top pocket. Andy and I walked over.

'Who dat?' Otis said and then sniffed. 'I smell a nasty old dog. That must be Andy. Tarka, girl, you ever think about giving your owner a bath?'

At the word bath, Tarka whined. We all laughed.

'This is Jack,' Andy said, motioning to me. 'He's looking for his daddy.'

'Hi,' I said.

There was a pause.

'Well, give him a poster,' Andy said impatiently.

Give a poster to a blind man? I thought. But Andy knew best. I got one out and slid it into Otis's hand.

Then Otis raised his dark glasses and peered at the page.

'Oh!' I said. 'I'm sorry. I thought you were...' and then wished I hadn't said anything.

Otis made a sound like, 'Shoo', waving his hand. 'Half them folks think I'm blind. Think you gotta be Ray Charles or somethin' to sing soul.'

Andy grinned. 'Yeah, but they give you extra money,' he pointed out, 'and you don't exactly let on. Look at the way you patted the air for your stool when you could *see* where it was.'

Otis spread his hands. 'If it makes them happy,' he said, 'I'd hate to go disappointing the punters.' Then he laughed. I'd never heard anyone with a laugh like that. It was rich and warm and full of naughtiness. It made me smile in spite of myself, in spite of everything that was going on in my life. And Andy was giggling like a fool.

'Is that what you call that music?' I asked. 'Soul?'

Otis looked at me with his mouth open. 'Is this boy for real?' he asked Andy, who shrugged. 'Ain't you never heard of Soul, boy?'

I shook my head.

'Ain't you never heard of James Brown?'

I shook my head again.

'Sam and Dave?'

And again.

Otis's voice was climbing in both pitch and volume. He was nearly squealing when he asked me, 'Ain't you never even heard of Aretha?'

'No,' I said. And then, 'Sorry.'

'Man alive!' Otis shook his own head from side to side. 'Mm, mm, mm. This old world keep getting sorrier and sorrier. I be glad I'm an *old* man. Soon be out of it.' He clucked his teeth.

'Well, before you pop your clogs,' Andy interrupted, 'could you take a look at that picture and tell us if you've ever seen the guy?'

Otis squinted at me and held the picture up against the light from the street lamp. 'Hell, yes. I seen this guy.'

'Where, Otis?'

'In the Garden Street Hostel. He was there maybe two, maybe three months back. I missed a night, though, and then he was gone.' Otis lowered his voice. 'I think I recall there was some kind of ruckus.'

'Have you seen him since?' I asked.

Otis shook his head and handed me back the poster. 'Naw,' he said. 'I'll bet me he's down by the river. There's some folks back there these days. You know, Andy, down them arches.'

'I know them,' Andy said. 'I know them all too well.'

St Margaret's clock rang. Eleven-thirty.

'I gotta go,' Andy said. 'We'll try down there tomorrow night, eh? But don't go without me!'

I said thanks again, but he was already gone.

'They lock that B&B at midnight,' Otis said. 'I got another half an hour at this place I'm staying, 'cause they know I do this gig.' But he was already starting to stack his stuff up.

I looked around, peering into the shadows. I didn't want to leave, didn't want to start that long walk home in the dark all by myself. I especially didn't want to run into any of those horrible kids. The puffa brothers or the thin girl.

'You got someplace to go, kid?' Otis asked me. 'You got someplace safe to sleep?'

And then I felt ashamed of myself again. Ashamed for worrying about a long walk when I had a warm bed and everything at the end of it. I mean, some people have real problems. I didn't exactly have real problems. I had food, after a fashion, and a place to stay, and clothes and everything like that.

So I nodded and said thanks again.

And then I turned and went back the way I had come. I walked so fast through downtown that I was almost running. I didn't see anyone. I was already tired by the time I got to the worst part of the hill and my legs felt like jelly every step. I took it slower that night and I only had to stop twice. It seemed easier, I suppose, because I knew I could do it.

The house was dark again. I'd start seriously worrying about my teeth, if this kept on, but before I knew it, the alarm was buzzing.

4.

Over Easy

It was starting to feel normal. The whole thing – sneaking in and out, feeling tired, not speaking to my mother. Even dealing with the horrible food she was giving me. That morning it was really runny eggs on toast and I just ate the white bits and whatever toast wasn't soaked in goo without a sigh and grabbed another apple on my way out. The grapefruit juice went down the sink again.

Mum was looking a whole lot happier. She was humming around the kitchen and once had to stop herself from breaking into song. Her honey-coloured hair was shiny and she had her make-up on and everything, all ready for work.

My mum is quite pretty. She's not very tall but she's nice and thin and when she's happy she kind of glows. She's happy most of the time. It takes a lot to get my mum down. I was surprised I'd managed it for as long as I had.

It was weird how I felt. I mean, I *knew* how horrible she was being – to me and to Dad. Especially to Dad. But at the same time, part of me was really pleased to see her shiny and pretty again, pleased to have the house smelling like lemons and the carpet all clean and everything.

Have you ever noticed things like that? Paradox, they call it – contradictions that are true. I both hated and loved my mother. It was like I was about food. I both was interested in (my mum would say 'obsessed by') nutrition and still wouldn't eat half the things I knew were good for me. It's like everything in the world is true and good and bad equally. Whenever I think about this kind of stuff, it makes my head hurt.

Richard and I were still getting along, though he was quieter than usual. I think what we usually talked about was Mum. I used to pass messages on and stuff. But of course, I wasn't doing that any more.

We got stuck in a bit of traffic where they were resurfacing the road and it got almost uncomfortable, how quiet it was in the car. Richard turned on the radio and fiddled with a couple of stations and then turned it back off again with a sigh.

I was thinking about everything that had happened the night before. So I asked him, 'Richard, do you know who James Brown is?'

'Was,' he corrected. 'I think he's dead.'

'Who was he?'

'James Brown, the hardest working man in show business,' he said, and he said it in this funny American accent like the one Otis used. It made me smile. 'He's a soul singer.' Richard started drumming the steering wheel with his thumbs. He sang, 'I feel good,' and then went, 'ba da ba da ba da ba,' like he was a backing track before singing, 'I knew that I would, yeah. I feeeeeeeeeel good...' He trailed off, embarrassed.

I couldn't help laughing. And after a second or

so, Richard laughed, too. He said, 'I really like that kind of stuff. I used to collect albums.' He looked sad for a moment. 'They're gone, now, but I have most of it on CD.'

And it suddenly struck me that I'd never seen his CDs. And the reason I'd never seen them was because I'd never even been to Richard's flat. I mentioned this and he said, 'Well, your mum and I always thought you'd be more comfortable if we stayed at yours.'

I said, 'Oh.' I mean, what *could* I say? I never thought about it, but Richard must have all kinds of things that he really liked at his flat, that he did without when he came over to ours. So I changed the subject. 'Sam and Dave?' I asked.

'Sure. Got their greatest hits last year. Rhino brought it out. It really kicks!'

'Aretha?'

'Franklin? She's the Queen of Soul!' We were still stuck behind this bread lorry, but Richard didn't look sad anymore. He was smiling like he was having a wonderful morning. He said, 'You know, when I feel really, really low, I can put on

Aretha and just the sound of her voice cheers me up.' He looked sideways at me.

At last it was our turn to go. This guy with a green paddle was waving frantically and Richard pulled back out on to the road. But he kept talking. He said, 'I could make you a CD. Burn a little compilation, if you'd like.'

I said, yeah, that I'd really like that. But my mind wasn't on our conversation any more. It was on school. Suddenly, I was really dreading it. I'd never been so underprepared in my whole life.

And it showed. I was like a mouse or something all morning. I didn't have anything to say about *Huckleberry Finn* because I'd barely even cracked the spine of my paperback copy. I didn't have anything to say about the new fluidity of class in second century Rome, because I'd stopped reading that particular piece of homework before I'd got to any mention of fluidity of class. And it was just lucky that we were talking about amino acids in science because I know a bit about that kind of thing anyway. But when, as a follow-up question, Mrs McCalbie asked how the frog experiment was going, I had to admit that I hadn't done the measurements since last Friday. Dill had to answer for me.

Anne's mouth just dropped open. And I knew I was for it. She's not the kind of girl to let something like that slide.

Now, I'd never really been part of a group before I started at this school. It had really surprised me how they were interested in everything about my life. And it had shocked me that Anne assumed she was in charge of me – that she could tell me what was and wasn't right or wrong in everything I did. As if because she acted like my friend, she now somehow *owned* me.

I was also surprised how much I didn't mind.

We're a bit of an odd bunch, and in my school, that's really saying something. We all started here in the middle of the year, for various reasons. Anne hated boarding at an even posher school. Dill came back from spending a year and a half with his grandparents in Jamaica. Scott's mum had been pulling her hair out, trying to get him a good education in state schools: our area had him in a Special Needs unit because of his cerebral palsy and he was so bored that he was getting depressed. She went back to work to pay the fees.

That's how expensive my school is – Scott's mum works just to pay his fees. I'm on a scholarship. Richard helped me study for the entrance exam and then we got help with the fees. We could never have afforded it otherwise. Even the uniform nearly breaks us.

Not like Dill and Anne. They're both rich. Dill's dad is in software design and Anne's family have just always had money.

I forgot Wesley. He was there already. He just hadn't ever really fitted into any other crowd.

So.

We eat lunch together and we go to movies and spend weekends together and stuff like that. And when I'm with them, the times I spend wondering whether or not they really like me seem silly. But when I'm not with them, I wonder. They're all such nice kids, from really good homes. I wonder if they're just being nice to me. It's the kind of thing they'd do.

Either way, I've known Anne long enough to realise that when she gives me that look, she's going to have a talk with me, whether I want it or not.

She cornered me at lunch. 'What is going on with you?' she asked, just like Scott had the day before. 'And don't give us any lame excuses.' Anne is going to be the managing director of the company they're planning to form, and she acts like one already.

Dill and Wesley arrived with their trays. Wesley had an extra tray, as well, which meant Scott was on his way. I waited until they all sat down, which gave me some time to think, because Scott always has to have a couple of goes at the benches before he manages to slide himself in.

Anne waited. She's good at that. She's good at almost everything, even sport. When I first started at this school, I thought they'd all be like Anne. She's posh. Talks posh and rides a pony. She even wears an Alice band, though she says her hair is so fair and so fine nothing else will keep it out of her eyes. She's pale as milk and her eyelashes and eyebrows are so white you can't even see them. That's what makes her eyes such a surprise.

Even with the extra time, I couldn't think of anything else to say. And I half wanted to see what they'd say if I told the truth. So I just came out with it. 'I'm looking for my dad.'

That shut them up for a long moment. Long enough for me to eat a couple of spoonfuls of goulash. I mean, ordinarily, I'd really avoid the school goulash. But with my mum's campaign to starve me out of resistance, it tasted pretty good and I was having a hard time concentrating on the conversation with it right under my nose, steaming at me.

Anne finally said, 'But isn't your dad a... isn't your dad homeless?'

You see what I mean? She'd probably started to say 'bum' or 'crusty' or something, but she's so nice, she changed it.

I nodded. 'That's why it's taking so long to find him.' I took a deep breath. 'I've been leaving the house at night and walking downtown.'

'What?' Anne screeched. Her prim little mouth gaped again. 'Jack, that's really dangerous!'

No one had ever called anything I did 'dangerous' before. It sounded great. Suddenly, I felt like it was cool, what I was doing, sneaking out of the house and everything. I felt like 007. So, naturally, I bragged. 'Well, I've made a couple of friends on the street, you know. They're giving me a hand.'

I looked round the table. Dill, Scott and Wesley were all sitting with their mouths hanging open.

Then they noticed me looking and shut their jaws. Scott lagged a little behind, but Dill and Wesley spoke at the same time.

Dill said, 'I want to come.'

Wesley asked, 'How do you get out?'

I answered Wesley. I said, 'It's easy. My mum's not speaking to me right now. So I just walk out. She thinks I'm in my room, asleep.'

'When do you leave the house?' Anne asked.

I shrugged, 'About ten, ten-ten thirty.' Wesley and Anne looked disapproving, but I could tell Dill thought it was really cool.

'So you *could* still do your work, then, couldn't

you, Jack?' Anne said, and she had a point. I suppose I could. I spent most of the time between tea and leaving just looking at the clock.

'Well, yeah...' I said.

'Well, you'd better do it,' she said, 'unless you *want* somebody to notice. Unless you *want* to get caught.' And she turned her amazing eyes on me. They're blue. Not pale and washy like mine, but real blue, blue like the sea. And sometimes they can bore right into you, just as they were right then. And I didn't know. *Did* I want to get caught? I still don't really know.

When I had started this, it had been on kind of a whim, and I thought I'd just do it the one night. I hadn't really thought about having to do it all the time and how to fit it in with the rest of my life. Anne's eyes were waiting for an answer. At last I said, 'Well, I will.' And it was nice to see how the hardness of her eyes seemed to melt.

'OK then,' she said softly. And then, 'Do you want my goulash?'

Scott had been pretty quiet for a change. But just as I took the first bite he said, 'I c-could nev-

never sneak out. M-m-my m-m-mum looks at me ev-every two seconds.'

'Mine, too,' Wesley said glumly.

'Mine doesn't.' Dill has three brothers and two sisters. His mum is really nice, but she doesn't have time to be as interfering as some of our mums are. I mean, my mum is pretty cool compared to the way most of the mums are at our school. It must be something about having a bright kid that makes them afraid for us. You could understand Scott's mum being that way, because he's got an illness. But Wesley doesn't have an illness and his mum is just as bad as Scott's. Even worse.

'I want to come,' Dill said again.

'It's not a game, Dill,' I said. 'It can get kind of scary.'

'All the more reason there should be two of us.' He grinned at me and Dill has this really nice grin. Out of all of us, he and Anne are the most nearly human. Even my mum thinks Dill is cute. But of course, Dill's famous grin doesn't work on me. I'm not a girl.

'Maybe tomorrow night. Not tonight, though.' And he seemed happy enough with that.

I thought, as I finished Anne's goulash, that maybe this was what would make me a really interesting person to have as a mate. I mean, Anne had that amazing house and the pony. Dill had all the latest games at his house and was the best-dressed boy in school. Scott had C. P. And Wesley...

Well, maybe Wesley didn't have anything cool that everyone liked him for. And I guess Scott's illness really isn't that much of a...

I don't know. I wanted a reason for them to like me. If they *did* like me. I wanted to be the streetwise one, or something. I wanted to have some reason to believe they were really my friends, something I could take with me, all the places I went.

I was going down to the arches that night. I knew that. I knew I needed every bit of belief I could get. I felt scared. So scared that I didn't finish Wesley's goulash and could barely even choke down Dill's.

5.

It's a Man's World

Something happened that night that made everything just that little bit easier. During dinner (broccoli and tofu stir-fry with ginger rice – I hate broccoli *and* ginger and I don't think anybody on earth likes tofu), Mum slid an envelope across the table to me.

I think at this point Mum was starting to enjoy our not talking to each other. I knew for sure she was starting to have fun thinking of different ways to gross me out with horrible meals.

I opened the envelope and it was pocket money. For last week and for this week. No note. Nothing else. Just a tenner and two fives. I nearly said, 'Thank you.' But I caught myself in time and just nodded.

That night I took the bus.

It felt strange to be on the bus so late. People were looking at me. I was the only person on it under thirty. Whenever anybody got on, they stared at me as they went past my seat, like they'd never even seen a child before. Walking, I reckon I'd have been more invisible.

I stayed invisible, all the way through town. Nobody grabbed me or bothered me. I passed Burger King. I passed Woolworths. I passed the Tesco Metro. Nothing. I didn't realise how tense I was until I saw Andy and Tarka. I could feel blood run back into my fingers and realised I'd been clenching my fists.

I was early. Andy was still selling to the people coming out of the cinema. Still, when he saw me, he started to pack up, 'We'd better go if you still want to. I've got to be home by midnight.'

'What about your customers?'

He shrugged. 'I've made enough money today. Tarka and I ate twice.'

I thought about this and took out one of my fivers. I said, 'Here. Take this, Andy. I don't want you to lose out.'

But that seemed to make him angry. He started shoving his things into his bag any old how. He was usually really careful and methodical. He said, 'I don't want your money.' He said it the way he'd spoken to me that first night, cold and harsh.

I mumbled, 'Sorry,' and folded up Tarka's blanket. He snatched it out of my hand and did it again himself. I couldn't see that he'd done it any better than I had. In fact, it was quite a bit worse.

I said, 'Sorry,' again, just standing there. I didn't know what else to say.

But something must have showed on my face, because Andy kind of sighed. He handed me back Tarka's blanket and went back through his bag, putting everything right while I folded it up properly again. He said, 'No mate, you're OK. It's just... I spent so much time begging money off people. That's all I wanted people for, money. I never had any real friends, I never did anything for anybody else. And now I can, I can do things for other people. See?'

I didn't really, but I nodded.

He sighed again. 'So I got angry at your money, see? 'Cause I'm doing this just to help *you*, not because you're a rich kid that I can get something out of.'

Now I really *did* see. But I said, 'I'm not rich, Andy.'

He shrugged. 'You don't look like you need anything to me.'

And as we walked along, I thought about that. I mean, there were tons of things I wanted. I had this old computer that still had Windows 95 on it, for goodness sakes, and I wanted one of the new Powerbooks. I wanted PlayStation 2. I wanted new trainers. And this time I wanted Nikes instead of those cut-price Reeboks that Mum had found at the supermarket. I wanted designer jumpers, not the ones Nana Burke knitted for me. I wanted a mobile phone.

But I didn't really need any of that stuff. Though pretty soon my computer was going to have to be either upgraded or replaced. But that was pretty soon. Not now. And I had nearly twenty quid in my pocket.

For the first time in my whole life, I realised that compared to a lot of people – maybe even compared to most people, I *was* rich.

We walked past the big pub and saw Otis doing his act. He was singing sad and slow to this really heavy rhythm on the karaoke machine, waggling his head back and forth like he was about to die from sadness. There was a crowd around him and they were all quiet, mesmerised.

Andy chuckled. 'That old man's gonna clean up tonight,' he said. 'He's got them eating out of the palm of his hand.'

I said, 'I really like that kind of music,' and Andy smiled.

He said, 'I realised something, watching Otis; poor black people make this great music and then all the rich white people buy it. And, like, the sadder or angrier it is, the more the white people eat it up with a spoon. It's pretty strange.'

I said, 'I've never been that interested in music.'

We were walking along streets of houses that were built a long time ago. Terraces. They'd probably been for poor people, too, but now posh folks lived in them. You could tell. There were lots of hanging baskets and no nets on the windows. You could see straight into some of them, see the polished wood tables and the big sofas.

Andy said, 'Well if you aren't interested in music, what *are* you interested in? What floats your boat, Jack? Besides searching for missing people, I mean.'

Before I even thought to censor it, I said, 'I'm quite into nutrition, actually. Especially food values. I do a lot of reading and research on the internet.'

Andy just stopped walking to stare at me. This brought Tarka up short so she looked up at me, too.

I could feel myself going red. I said, 'Ummm,' but it wasn't like I could *explain* myself or anything.

Then Andy laughed. I don't think I'd ever seen him really laugh before. He had this funny high-pitched giggle. It made Tarka bark. He bent over, holding his side and Tarka kind of jumped around him, licking his ears while he just lost it.

'Heee!' he finally said, shaking his head. 'Jack Burke, you're an odd character, no doubt about it.' He settled his bag back on his shoulder and rubbed his ribs. 'I haven't laughed so hard for...' But he trailed off. He must have seen how uncomfortable I was.

'Come on.' Andy put his arm around my shoulder.

His jumper smelled stale. 'Let's go and find this dad of yours.'

We walked over an old humpbacked canal footbridge and it was like some sort of secret portal to another world. Behind us were the rows of orderly houses with everything all nice – winter pansies in baskets and shiny cars parked outside on the cobbled street.

In front of us was a wasteland of huge gas canisters, train tracks and low metal buildings behind sagging chain-link fences. Behind some of the fences, dogs snarled. The pavement gave out gradually, changing to tarmac and then to a narrow dirt path between banks of overgrown weeds.

I slowed down, stumbling in the dark, but Andy and Tarka just kept walking, as if they'd done it a thousand times, as if they knew every pebble on the path by feel alone. We walked towards the dark arches under the railway bridge.

You could smell them before you could see them. Part of it was what they were burning – anything they could find – in big old metal drums.

But part of it was the men themselves. They smelled terrible, of dried sweat and wee and sick. The first man we saw had a big overcoat with vomit all down the front of it and stuck into his beard. He roared something at Andy, who just waved, as if that was a perfectly reasonable greeting from a perfectly ordinary person. I found myself holding on to Andy's arm, but even when I realised what I was doing, I couldn't bring myself to let go.

'Don't worry,' he said. 'Some of them are more normal than others. We're going to talk to the more normal ones.'

The more normal ones had their fire up against a brick wall. There were five or six of them, all wearing great big overcoats and some of them had blankets around their shoulders as well. They smelled bad, too, but not as bad as the others had done. Their eyes were all red, with the smoke, I guessed. They stood or sat against the brick wall on old chairs with legs missing, propped up on bricks, or with backs missing and leant up against the wall.

Andy walked right up to them and nodded at the biggest one, who was sitting where the fire was warmest on the plumpest of the chair remains. He said, 'Dave.'

And Dave said, 'Andy.'

There was no emotion in their voices at all. No 'great to see you' sound. No 'I'm really surprised you're here' sound. Nothing. Nothing at all.

There was a long moment while they looked at each other.

Everyone had kind of stopped whatever they were doing to watch, as if this was a momentous occasion or something. Andy put his hand on my shoulder and said, 'This is Jack. He's looking for his dad.'

By now, I didn't need telling. I took one of my posters out of the carrier bag and handed it to Dave. He looked at me before he looked at the poster. His eyes were red and piggy and colder than the night. He looked at me for even longer than he'd looked at Andy. Then he looked at Andy again before he finally, finally looked at my poster.

He snorted. 'You didn't need me for this,' he said. 'Anybody could have told you. John Burke is right over there.'

6.

Until you come back to me (that's what I'm gonna do)

'Over there' was a heap of blankets against the wall. Not just by the fire, but not all that far away, either. It wasn't until we walked right over that I could see there was someone inside it.

Andy just nodded at me, one of those 'go on' kind of nods. I hesitated, but then walked forwards. Tarka whined, as if she didn't want me to go and I hesitated again.

But Andy said, 'Go on, Jack. We've only got a couple of minutes.'

And so I went.

He wasn't asleep, but he wasn't far off it. His

eyes opened when I got close to him. They were red and piggy, just like everyone else's there.

I bent down over him. He smelled bad, sick.

I said, 'Dad?'

And he said, 'Jack?' and blinked a couple of times. He rubbed his face with his hand. The nails were black around the edges. He said, 'Jack?' again and this time his voice sounded a bit stronger.

'Yeah,' I said. 'It's me.' But I was thinking, how could she do this? How could the mum I knew, the mum who sold her car to buy my first computer, the mum who worked all day and yet still managed to have the house tidy and tea ready when I came home from school, the mum who up until a week ago came into my room to kiss me goodnight every night of my life – how could *that* mum do this to anyone, let alone someone she had loved?

'Thank God,' Dad said. 'Have you got any money on you, Jack?'

I had to listen to this replay in my head a couple of times before I understood it. But Dad went on to say, 'It's just that I'm sick, Jack, really sick.' He coughed, a wet claggy cough that seemed to shake his whole body. 'Sick,' he repeated while he coughed. 'And I need some medicine.'

'How much is it?'

Dad looked me over with his red eyes. His face was red, too, especially his nose, and rough. He'd been overexposed to the weather, that much was sure. And it looked like he had a vitamin C deficiency as well as probably being anaemic. He had that feverish paleness that comes with lack of iron. He said, 'A fiver? Have you got a fiver, Jack?'

I reached into my coat pocket and took out the five pound note which Andy had refused and pushed it into his hand.

'God bless you, son,' Dad said, and smiled. I wished he hadn't. His breath was horrible and his teeth were matted in plaque.

Andy said, 'We've got to go now, Jack.'

I felt like I couldn't leave my dad that way, just lying there. 'I'll stay,' I said.

'No you won't.' Andy's voice was firm. 'You'll come with me. Now.'

'Meet me tomorrow night,' I said to my Dad. 'Meet me outside Burger King downtown. I'll buy you some good food.' Then I looked at him again. 'Do you think you can make it that far?'

But Dad had perked up a little. He was sitting up now, leaning against the wall. He said, 'I'll be there, son. I'll be there.'

I didn't know what to do. I half wanted to hug him, but I just... couldn't. And he didn't make any move to touch me.

So we just nodded at each other. And then I went.

I couldn't see the path at all on the way back. My eyes were full of tears. Andy was walking fast, Tarka trotting beside him. I tried to keep up but finally had to say that I couldn't.

Andy apologised as he slowed back down. He said, 'Jack, I know he's your dad, but you have to be careful, you know what I mean, mate?'

By now, we were passing the gas canisters and could see each other's faces by the security lights from one of the low metal buildings. I don't know what he saw in my face, but I could see that he looked really, really worried.

I said, 'What's wrong, Andy?'

But he just kind of muttered to himself as he walked. Finally, he said, 'OK, look.' We had stopped on the bridge. He held up a finger. 'Rule One,' he said. 'You don't come down here without me and Tarka.'

'Not even if my dad brings me?'

'Never. Not even with just me. Only with me *and* Tarka.'

I had no idea why this was, but Andy had been right about everything so far, so I nodded. 'OK,' I said. It wasn't much of a promise, but it *was* a promise. I'd like to say, looking back, that I never promised, but that would be a lie. I did and Andy knew I did.

'Two,' he said, holding up another finger. 'I want you to keep track of everything you give your dad and just what he does with it.'

'What do you mean?'

'Just do it, OK?'

We started walking again. Otis was packing up by the time we got to the big pub. Andy looked at the clock tower on the church and cursed. 'I'm going to have to run for it,' he said. 'But don't forget what I told you, Jack! Don't forget!'

He and Tarka were gone.

Otis was curling up an extension lead that came from the pub kitchen door. I curled up his mike lead for him the same way. He had little twisty tie things that made them all neat. He stacked everything, even his folding stool, on to a luggage trolley.

I said, 'How'd you do tonight, Otis?'

And he laughed his wicked laugh. He said, 'I made out like a bandit, Jack. You find your daddy yet?'

'Yeah. I found him.'

Otis looked at me for a second. He said, 'You be careful, son. People have a way of changing sometimes. I ought to know.' Then he said, 'You still got a good place to stay?'

I nodded.

'You'd better get off there, then. It's late.'

I thanked him and started for my bus stop. It was along the back of the big shops, Marks and Spencers, British Home Stores. There was a little alleyway that cut through. Just as I got to the end of the alleyway, I saw the thin girl again.

She was standing near the bus stop, under a lamp post, so you could see her really well. I shivered, just looking at her in her short skirt and bare legs. Her feet looked uncomfortable, too, in those high heels. You could see where they'd rubbed her raw.

Nobody should be that thin. I was sure she had an eating disorder. And then as I watched, she lit a cigarette. I thought to myself, now that won't help. Nicotine is an appetite suppressant. She wouldn't get as hungry as she should be if she was smoking. She'd get even thinner. Not to mention the cancer.

She didn't seem frightening, while I was watching her. She seemed younger and weaker. I was actually going to go and talk to her when a car pulled up and the two boys in puffa jackets got out. The three of them huddled together, sharing her cigarette and talking in low voices.

Something about them seemed really sad. Not sad as in pathetic, but sad as in unhappy. I didn't want to talk to them. I didn't want to even look at them any more. Something about the way they were standing together made my throat hurt, the way it does before you cry.

I walked home instead. Took it really slowly up the hill and only had to stop once.

I remembered the three of them standing on that corner when I woke up. Remembered how sad it had made me feel, watching them.

And then I remembered something else. It was Friday. Richard would be coming over. And he and Mum would get videos and a takeaway. They'd be in the lounge all night. There was no way I was going to be able to sneak out.

And my poor sick father would be waiting for me.

7.

What a Fool Believes

By the time I had showered and dressed, I knew I was going to have to talk to my mother. Still, I stayed upstairs five minutes after my usual breakfast time. I just couldn't face her.

It was even worse down in the kitchen. She had given me muesli with natural yoghurt. The muesli seemed to be made out of mainly hazelnuts (which I hate) and dust. The yoghurt wasn't the creamy kind – it had slimy, watery bits around the edges. I also had another grapefruit juice.

I sighed when I sat down in front of it. The only way to handle this, I thought, was to let her think she'd won. She was having another shiny, happy day. Her hair was all done up on top of her head and she wore this tan-coloured jumper that really suited her. The silver earrings Richard had given her for her birthday dangled against her neck.

She was just sitting there, drinking coffee at our nice, clean kitchen table in our nice, warm kitchen.

And my dad was waking up dirty against a cold brick wall under the railway arches. Sick. And hungry.

Suddenly, it was easy to lie to her. I said, 'Don't forget I'm staying over at Dill's tonight.'

Her eyes widened when I spoke, but she managed to stay cool, though she let a little glint of victory come into her eyes. She said, 'Oh, that's right. Thanks for reminding me.'

I got up and scraped my muesli into the bin and poured my grapefruit juice down the sink. It hurt to see her happy, thinking she'd won, thinking things were all better between us. I felt worse about making her happy than I ever had done making her miserable. At least when I made her miserable I was being honest.

She said, 'Look, have some peanut butter

toast before you go to school,' and my stomach turned over. Guilt, I guess.

But just then Richard pipped his horn and I didn't have to answer. I just grabbed my satchel and ran out the door.

In the car, Richard held up his hand for silence. Then he punched a button.

The sound was so loud I couldn't believe it. I'd ridden in his car hundreds of times but had no idea he had such an amazing system. There was this big, twanging bass noise, really heavy rhythm. Then this woman's voice screeched into my right ear, 'WHAT you want, baby I got it. WHAT you need, you know I got it. All I'm asking... is for a little RESPECT.'

Richard was nodding his head like it was on a string. He shouted, 'Aretha' to me. I let the bass and the horns pour through my chest and take me to another, a better place. A place with soul.

I looked around our lunch table. All of them had stopped eating and were sitting with their mouths open, even Anne. I finished telling them about the night before, saying, 'and then I had to go.'

'I ju-just don't be-be-be-be*lieve* this,' Scott shook his head so hard his glasses nearly came off.

Of course, Anne saw the problem straight away. 'But how will you get out of the house on a weekend night?' she asked, her blue eyes narrowing. 'Won't Mr Leakey be there?'

I looked at Dill. I said, 'I told my mum I was spending the night with you. Do you think I actually could?'

Dill smiled his cheekiest grin. 'Only if I get to come out with you.'

'Deal,' I said and we shook on it.

'Isn't that a bit short notice?' Wesley asked. 'I mean, won't your mum say no, Dill?'

Dill rolled his eyes at Wesley. 'I'll tell her we fixed it up weeks ago. She won't remember if we did or we didn't.'

I sighed with relief. I wasn't going to let my dad down, after all. He wouldn't be waiting there, cold, sick and hungry. I'd be there. And I'd take care of him.

*

Richard was happy as he drove me and Dill back to my place to pick up some stuff. My mum was happy to pack it all up for me. Dill's mum was happy to see me. Dill was practically jumping out of his skin with excitement about sneaking out.

The only one who wasn't happy was me. I was nervous, and kind of afraid of doing something wrong and letting my father down.

After tea (pizza and salad with proper lettuce, the first decent meal I'd had in ages), Dill and I went up into his room, the one he shared with Josh. Josh was visiting their auntie, so we had it to ourselves. We updated our internet pages on the frog research and checked out the site comments. One was from a graduate student at Stanford in California who said that we showed 'amazing insight and initiative' and that made us giddy. We flew around the room being Captain Insight and Initiative Man for a while. Then we collapsed on to the beds.

It had been dark for some time, and when I looked at Dill's clock, it was nearly nine. I decided we should go, and that I should do some shopping at the Tesco Metro before I met my dad, so he wouldn't have to trail around. I didn't remember much about him, but I remembered that he hated trailing around shops. And anyway, it was just as well that we got down there early so that we could take the bus without people staring at us.

Dill led the way. He went down into the living room and asked his dad if he had a spare diskette. Dill's dad was sitting with his feet up on the sofa, leaning against Dill's mum. They both looked exhausted. His dad kind of just motioned towards the next room and Dill closed the door.

The next room was his dad's study and usually off limits to Dill and his brothers and sisters. It had big French windows that led to the back garden. Dill undid the locks on these and when we closed them behind us, we didn't lock them again. We just jumped up on the wall at the end of the garden and walked along the top to the end of the street. It was easy.

Taking the bus was easy, too. Nobody stared

at us at all. I suppose it was more normal for there to be two of us. It was nice to have Dill along, though we weren't saying much.

At one point I turned to him and said, 'There's these kind of rough kids that hang out down there. I hope they don't bother us.'

Dill looked at me. His eyes seemed even bigger than normal. But he didn't say anything.

He stuck close to me as I got off at the right stop and walked to the pedestrianised section. There were a lot of people about.

We went into Tesco Metro and I got a bag of things that you could eat anywhere – you know, that you wouldn't have to cook or mix up or anything. Those little orange juice cartons with the straws attached for the vitamin C. Pre-sliced bread rolls for energy. Some cooked meats from the deli counter for protein and iron. Some soft cheese with chives – more protein. A salad pack that included baby spinach (you really can't taste it if it's *baby* spinach) – more iron. These nice yoghurt packs with crunchy cereal and fruit which were vitamin D enriched, as even though Dad was living outdoors, it didn't look like he was getting much sun. Bananas, for the potassium, to fight off depression.

It came to about ten pounds. I had just enough left for Dad's medicine and to buy him a coffee at Burger King. But we were still early.

Andy and Tarka were at their pitch and Andy was doing really well. He had a new issue of the *Big Issue* to sell and he was truly going for it. The earflaps on his mad hat were flapping as he ran from one side of the street to the other, catching groups coming from the cinema, the pubs, and the Italian restaurant. In every group, someone almost always bought one. Even Tarka was sitting up, smiling and wagging her tail, as if she knew the difference between how much Andy usually sold and how much he was selling that night. I thought maybe she knew there was a possibility of a fish supper on the way home.

Dill wanted to meet Andy, but I didn't want to interrupt him when things were going so well.

Instead, we walked down to the big pub around the corner and listened to Otis for a while. When we went back, Andy was still selling like mad. But I could see someone standing outside Burger King. I asked Dill if he'd mind waiting around Andy's pitch and kind of waved at Andy and pointed at Dill. Andy nodded to us both, and that seemed to make Dill feel a little more confident, though he did ask, 'What about the rough kids?'

I told him, 'Don't speak to them.' I left him sitting on a bench and went to meet my father.

He'd showered and he had on some clean clothes and a warm jumper. He'd bundled his big overcoat under his arm, though, and I could smell it as I got close. I said, 'Let's get a coffee,' as if it was the kind of thing I said every day. We went into Burger King and he found a table while I went up to order. I got myself a small coke, too. My mouth was dry.

When I got to the table, he had a moment to put the milk in and stir it around before he had to look at me. So I looked at him.

His eyes were still red and puffy and his skin seemed stretched and thin. His stomach was distended. Maybe it was fat, but I doubted it, because his shoulders were really thin. He was in a terrible state, really he was.

I passed over the carrier bag. I said, 'There's some good food in there.'

He said, 'Oh,' and had a drink of his coffee. And then he said, 'I thought you'd just give me the money and let me shop. How do you know what I like?'

I went red. I felt terrible. I wanted to say something about saving him the bother, but nothing came out. Instead, I pulled out the fiver I had left and slid it across the table.

My father's eyes lit up when he saw it.

'For your medicine,' I said.

'Ah, yes, my medicine,' he echoed. He pushed the money into his pocket, smiling at me. He said, 'You're a good boy, son.'

And I blushed again. He took a long drink of his coffee, but his eyes never left mine. He said, 'You turned out all right. In spite of your mother's mollycoddling. Coming out in the dark to see your old dad. Not many sons would do it, you know. You're one in a million.'

A strange, warm feeling filled my chest. I tried to drink some of my coke, but I felt like it was choking me. He was waiting for me to say something. I said, 'I'm worried about you.'

He smiled with half his mouth. 'Don't you worry about me, son,' he said. 'I know how to look after myself. I've *had* to look after myself. Ever since your mother took me for everything I had and threw me out on the streets.' His red eyes narrowed. 'How is the bitch?' he asked.

I didn't like to hear that word. But it made me think about that morning, how she'd sat with her silver earrings at the table all shiny and warm, drinking out of the Wedgwood cup she'd found at a car boot sale. And how I was sitting there with my dad, and how he was drinking out of a paper cup, his overcoat stinking under the table. It wasn't right. It just wasn't right.

I shrugged.

'She'll be fine, that one,' Dad said bitterly. 'She

always knew best. She's probably got some other poor soul dancing to her tune now. Doesn't she?'

I didn't say anything.

'Doesn't she?' he asked, louder. The people at the next table looked.

I nodded. 'Yeah,' I said. 'She's engaged.'

'Engaged?' Dad's lip curled up again in his half smile. And then his expression changed. 'And here I am, alone,' he coughed. 'Dying for all anyone cares.'

'What's wrong with you?' I asked. 'What is this medicine you have to take every day?'

'Oh, I don't want to talk about that, son.' Dad smiled bravely. 'If I had a little more money, maybe I could get that test done but... no. Let's not talk about it. Let's talk about the good times, eh? When we had a proper family. Do you remember when I used to take you to Highbury? To see the Gunners? Those were the days.'

'Yeah,' I said, but all I really remembered was a vague feeling of panic. I changed the subject. 'What are you working on?' I asked.

I didn't think he understood, so I explained.

'Your letter. It said you were working hard. I just wondered what—'

'I can't tell you,' Dad interrupted, looking around. 'It's secret. And anyway...' he went off into another fit of coughing, '...I'm too sick right now to do too much. To think for the price of a seat these days at Highbury I could...' he trailed off, sniffling.

'How much do you need?' I asked. 'I've got some money saved.'

He coughed some more. 'I couldn't take money from you, son,' he said.

But I was soon able to persuade him. We agreed to meet the next night down at the arches. He seemed a bit dazed by the warmth and the coffee and the conversation. When we stood up to go, I had to remind him to take the carrier bag of food.

At the door, he stopped and put his hand on my shoulder, as if he was going to pull me to him. But he didn't. He just kind of patted me. Then he took off down the alleyway, down some short cut I guessed. And I went to find Dill.

Dill had a stack of *Big Issues* in his arms and was following Andy around, so that Andy didn't have to keep going back to his pitch every time he sold a few. Andy was still selling like mad. I'd never seen him do so well. Tarka was really excited. I went over to see her and she jumped up and gave me a nuzzle behind my ear. Then she licked me all down my cheek, which was a bit gross, to be honest, but because it was her, I didn't really mind.

I didn't really mind anything. I was almost numb from feeling, from feeling too much. My Dad thought I was great – that I was one in a million. Every time I remembered his words I couldn't swallow. I just stood there for a while, watching Andy and Dill work, too full to speak, too full to even breathe properly.

8.

Chain of Fools

'No.' It was all he kept saying. I couldn't believe it.

'But, Andy—' I started again.

'No.' He stopped packing up his stuff and put his mittened hand on my shoulder. In spite of what a great night he'd had, his eyes looked really tired and sad. He said, 'Jack, I should never have taken you down there in the first place. It's not right. And I don't want you to go down there again.'

He really wouldn't do it. He wouldn't take me down to the arches on Saturday night. 'But I promised my dad!' I half shouted. 'He needs the money!'

'Money?' Andy let go of me and shook his head. 'You gave him more of your money?'

'He needs it,' I said. 'He needs this test.'

Andy rolled his eyes. 'I thought you kids were supposed to be clever,' he said. He looked at me again. Goodness knows how I looked to him. I was fighting back tears. 'Go home, Jack. Forget all about this. Forget about your dad. Forget about me and Otis. Just go home with your mate, here.'

He gave me a little push and turned and started packing up his pitch. I looked at Dill and Dill shrugged. He didn't know what had gone wrong, either.

All I said was, 'But—'

But Andy looked at me again, and this time, there was that same anger in his eyes I'd seen the other night. He said, 'Look, Jack, I made a mistake. I made a bad mistake. And you've got to help me to put it right. And the way you can do that is to *go home*. And *stay* there. And live right and eat your greens and all that stuff. So if you really think we're mates at all, *please*, *please* just go and do that. Now.'

His face was all sweaty and he looked like his patience was exhausted.

'Hello, Andy. How's business?'

A man was standing there. I mean, was *just standing there*. One second it was the three of us and the next he'd just appeared, like he'd been beamed there or something.

I jumped and so did Dill. Andy didn't. He said, 'And here's the Countess, to make my night complete.'

The man bared his teeth. They were white, almost too white. He was thin and tall and wore a long black coat that looked very warm. It had a fur collar. He smelled of some expensive scent, not really too much of it, but nearly. When he showed his teeth, it wasn't anything like a smile. He said, 'Call me Roger, Andy.'

Andy sighed. 'What do you want, *Countess*?' he said and folded his arms across his chest. Tarka rumbled in her throat.

'Ah, the little doggums,' the Countess said. His eyes were dark and cold. They flicked over Tarka to me, where they rested for a moment. I had to stop myself from shivering.

'You aren't doing anything else but the day job, are you, Andy?'

'No!' Andy was emphatic. 'I just sell the paper.'

The Countess waved his hands over mine and Dill's head. He had dark purple gloves, leather. 'And these?' he asked.

'Friends,' Andy said. 'You wouldn't know about that.'

'No.' The Countess' voice was flat. He looked at Andy for a long time. 'And that's all you know?'

'That's all I'm telling.'

Then the Countess did something really creepy. He bent over to look in my eyes. I could feel him measuring me in some way. 'Who's Richard?' he asked.

'Don't tell him anything,' Andy said. But he didn't need to. I couldn't speak.

'I'll see you again, young man,' the Countess said, straightening. 'You can be sure of it, Andy dear.'

I watched him take one, two steps away. But then he was gone again, first in a shadow and then simply not there any more. Tarka gave a short bark after him. Then she shivered, settling her fur back down.

I looked at Dill and Dill looked at me.

'Do you see what I mean?' Andy said. 'Can't you see what I mean?' He looked as if he was about to cry. 'Will you please, *please* just go home, both of you? Push off. Now.'

Then *he* got down and looked at me. 'Please.' His eyes were worried. Tarka whined and came to lean against my leg, as if she was asking me, too.

I said, 'OK, Andy. Whatever you say,' and I could see the relief in his face.

And then Dill and I just sort of mumbled goodbye and left. Of course, I hadn't meant what I'd said. But what else could I do?

The next morning, I woke up in Dill's room and thought about it some more. I still couldn't make any sense of it.

I lay there, thinking. I kept wondering about the Countess, just why he was so interested in me. And why the whole thing made Andy so frightened.

And I remembered...

My dad is holding my mum by the back of her neck. It's like they're dancing, but there isn't any music. Their feet are going slap, slap, on the kitchen lino. I must be sitting on the floor, but I don't know why. I'm old enough to walk. I don't know how I know that, but I do.

Then Mum says, 'Let Jack leave the kitchen.'

And Dad laughs. It's not a very nice laugh, in fact, it's a horrible laugh, not really a laugh at all, more of a crow. He pushes Mum's head down really hard. She struggles to get away. He pushes it again and she butts her head in his stomach.

This makes him angry. He stops smiling.

He looks at me. 'Are you watching?' he says. And then...

Marcia, one of Dill's little sisters ran in and jumped on me, shouting, 'Jack! Jack!'

I blinked. The memory evaporated like steam.

'Do you want to play Barbies?'

I said, 'Um.' I was trying to hold on to the memory. It was important, I could tell.

'Bog off, Marcie. We just woke up!' A pillow

came sailing across the room, heading pretty accurately for Marcia's head. She dodged it no problem, sticking out her tongue.

'I like Jack better than you, Dillon Francis. You know why, Dillon Francis? Because Jack is nice and you are horrid.'

Dill's mum came in then. 'Marcia, you go and do something to that hair. You've got four minutes. Dillon, wash your smelly little butt and pack your footie kit. It's Saint Gerrard's boys today. Jack, love, I made your favourite breakfast. Why don't you come down while the tomatoes are still warm?'

Before I knew it, Richard was pipping his horn and I was off home. I never had time to work it out in my head at all.

I thought if I could just lie down for a few moments, I might be able to figure everything out. But I'd forgotten all about Scouts.

I forgot like you forget when you don't want to remember. There was this coach trip to go walking that I'd been dreading, and so I just forgot about it. I think I used to do that a lot. Mum and Richard, however, had remembered.

They'd decided, about a year before, that I had to do *something* physical. I was hopeless at games, and so they'd signed me up for this particular Scout troop that did a lot of rambling. Richard had gone to university with the Scoutmaster. As the alternative was something even more ghastly, like gymnastics or something, I had reluctantly agreed.

So I got home on Saturday morning just in time to shower and get my stupid shirt and scarf and hat on. I also had these shorts. With my big boots, they made my legs look even thinner. I really couldn't bear to look at myself in my Scouts outfit. It was depressing.

Mum had packed a lunch for me in her old backpack and Richard drove me down to the church hall where we all met.

I didn't have any friends there, really, but there were a couple of equally weedy geeks that I always got stuck with. They sat together, though, on the coach and I was on a seat by myself. The

Scoutmaster was this jolly guy who loved show tunes. He had us singing 'Oklahoma' before we even hit the motorway.

I couldn't think at all, singing. And it was impossible not to sing. He had all the words on big bits of card and always noticed. So I sang.

I mean, everything had gone wrong. And I really didn't know what I was going to do. I didn't know how I was going to get out of the house and I didn't know how I was going to get down to the arches and I didn't know what I'd done to make Andy not want to help me any more. Life seemed pretty hopeless.

And having to sing 'Oh, What a Beautiful Morning' and 'Surrey with a Fringe on Top' didn't really help.

When we got to the beginning of the walk, I was ready for the pain. I know I spend too much time behind a keyboard and don't get enough exercise. I know because our PE teacher is always telling me that. And I know that the reason my legs hurt walking up stairs is because my cardio-pulmonary efficiency is low and can't shift the lactic acid my muscles make when they move. I know that this will lead to heart problems in later life if I don't do something about it now. It's just that everything you can do about it is equally boring and painful.

I started down the trail while most people were still pulling their socks up and fiddling with their packs. I usually did head off first on these things, so that I wouldn't be too far behind by the time everyone else passed me by.

But something strange happened.

I suppose it was all the walking around I'd been doing every night. But I went down the path and then even up a pretty steep hill, and my legs didn't ache at all. I got a bit winded, but I just unzipped my jacket and let the cold air hit my chest and was able to keep going. Nobody had passed me. I walked to the top of the next hill and then the next one and then the next one. That was the highest point.

There was a break in the trees and all of a sudden I could see for miles, a clear, unbroken horizon. Houses and walls and sheep and green fields were laid out below me like toys on a rumpled blanket. There was a big rock there and I sat on it. The wind was getting up, but I was a bit sweaty and it felt good to me. The air tasted clean, almost minty. Or maybe that was my toothpaste. I don't know.

What I do know is that for the few minutes I was sat there, I didn't think about anything. Not about my mum and the letters. Not about Richard. And not about Dad. I had this strange feeling of being kind of suspended, as if my brain was switched off for repairs or something.

And when some of the others and the Scoutmaster caught up with me and said it was time to eat our sandwiches, I found I was starving.

On the coach back, while my mouth was singing 'Consider Yourself At Home', my brain started working overtime. Of course, the only answer was that I had to tell Mum and Richard what was going on.

I always said I was nearly thirteen, but really my birthday was months away. I was only twelve years old, for goodness' sake. There's only so much a twelve-year-old could do on their own.

And then Richard could find out about Mum and the letters and my Mum could find out that Dad was really sick, and surely, *surely*, they could all come to some sort of a solution better than my dad sleeping against a wall under the railway arches. I could pay for the test and maybe we could get Dad well and then... who knows what might happen then? Maybe he and Mum would get together again.

Which wasn't really nice for Richard, but better than Mum lying to him, not telling him about the letters and crying about my dad.

It was going to be a terrible scene. I'd probably be grounded for life. But it had to be done.

I was all ready to do it when the coach dropped off four or five of us on my estate and I walked up to the house. I took a deep breath and twisted the kitchen door handle. It didn't open, so I twisted it again. And then I stared at it for a second, before I got my key out and opened it. I just couldn't believe that it was locked.

The house was quiet and dark, except for the light in the kitchen. There was a note on the table. It said, 'Sweetie, we have to go out. There's lasagne in the oven and a salad in the fridge.' And that was it.

I took off my muddy boots and went upstairs to change. And then I just lay on the bed for a moment.

I mean, I'd been all set to tell Richard and my mum everything, and then they weren't there to tell. I was all set to be open and honest and mature and reasonable. But then this opportunity to do it my own way was just given to me.

And I couldn't resist it.

It was after 8.30. I got my roll of money out from its hiding place in my sock drawer and stuffed it in the pocket of my jeans. I wiped the mud off my boots with kitchen towel. And then I let myself out of the house. I didn't eat the lasagne. I didn't eat the salad. It was as if I'd forgotten all about food, like my stomach didn't even exist any more.

*

I'd walked just far enough to know that my legs were going to hurt the next day when Dill jumped down off a garden wall on to the path in front of me.

'What are *you* doing here?' I asked him.

'I knew you'd go down to the arches tonight,' he said. 'I knew you'd find some way to go.' He grinned. 'I'm coming, too.'

There was nothing I could say to stop him. He even had our bus fare. I was glad of the company, though I wondered why he was coming along. Was it because he wanted to support me? Or was it because it was more exciting than whatever was happening at home?

We got off at the usual stop and walked down through the pedestrianised section. When we got near Andy's pitch, we stayed close to the shopfronts, even ducking down the mouths of the alleys. In one of them, Dill saw this carrier bag from Tesco's and started looking through it.

'Leave it!' I hissed, eager to get past Andy before he saw us.

But Dill said, 'It's your dad's bag.' I went over and looked. And it was. Everything was still in there – the bananas were all spotty with frost, and the salad bag looked pretty sad, but the rolls, the meat, the juices... even the nice yoghurty things... they were all still in the bag. I looked at Dill and he shrugged. He said, 'Maybe it was too heavy for him to carry.'

Maybe. But something about it made my chest feel tight, and that warm feeling I'd had about doing the right thing was gone.

I looked out of the alleyway and could see Andy's back, could see the lump at his feet I knew was Tarka. Andy wasn't working as hard as he usually did, he was just kind of standing there, a bit saggy. I wanted to go and talk to him and find out if he was all right. But I couldn't.

Instead, I led Dill down past the big pub – where I could just hear Otis singing something about the dock of a bay – down to the nice cobbled terrace. And then we crossed over the canal bridge into the wasteland that led to the arches.

9.

Greenbacks

Dill stumbled going down the path and grabbed my arm to steady himself. Then he just didn't let it go. When the first dog launched itself against the wire fence we were passing, slavering and growling, I could hear Dill make this little whimpering sound. He was already scared and we still had the less normal ones to get through.

I stopped walking. I said, 'Look, Dill, why don't you wait on the bridge for me?'

He said, 'No, it's OK.' But he didn't walk on. We looked at each other as best we could in the yellow glow of the warehouse security lights. I couldn't see much of his face, but I could tell by the way he stood that he didn't know what to do.

So I said, 'No, really. You wait back there.'

But he said, 'I didn't know it was going to be like this, Jack. I don't think you should go down there. It's well scary.'

We were just where the tarmac ends. I swallowed, thinking of the less normal ones. But I tried to sound confident when I said, 'Wait on the bridge. I'll be OK.' And I kept walking.

What happened next seems to have happened really fast. It didn't feel it that night, but when I look back at it, I can't remember a lot. And then, I suppose, I didn't really know everything that was happening at the time. But I'm not going to break my promise to you. You'll get the whole truth. I've spoken to everybody about it and I think I'm ready to try and tell it properly.

So.

No one was waving a stick or on fire or anything when I passed the less normal ones. They just huddled around their fire barrel. They looked at me, but they didn't say anything or do anything. I remember thinking that was a good sign. It just shows you, doesn't it, how when you start going really wrong, you get everything else wrong as well.

When I got to the bit of the wall where Dave's fire was, I could see Dave and my dad. There were five or six other men there, too, some of them a lot younger – Andy's age. There was a pile of timber next to the fire that I thought was fuel.

My dad smiled at me. He was clean again and his teeth were brushed. To get to him, I had to walk into the circle of other men. They all looked at me, but none of them looked in my eyes. I could feel them move back into a closed circle when I got inside by the fire.

I hugged my dad. I hadn't before, and I don't really know why I did then. His body went all stiff and awkward when I put my arms around him. He patted me, but kind of like you would a car or a table or something, not like one human being to another. Close to, he smelled of alcohol.

A lot.

And I remembered...

I'm back in the kitchen, watching my mum and dad. She asks him if I can go, but he says no again. He smells of alcohol.

She tries to get away, but he's holding her by the back of the neck. He's a lot bigger than she is. A lot. I never really thought about that before.

She butts him in the stomach, trying to loosen his hold, but although he gets more angry, he doesn't let her go.

He looks right at me and his eyes are the coldest things I've ever seen. He says, 'Are you watching?'

And of course I am, though I wish I wasn't.

Then with one hand, he brings my mother's face down hard on to the kitchen table. It makes this wet, slapping sound. He pushes her neck down and down on one side. Her face is getting pushed all around, the skin folding up in ways it shouldn't.

When he lets her up, I realise I hadn't been breathing.

Then he slams her down again. He wraps his fingers further around her neck. She's not breathing properly. She opens her mouth, gasping. Her face is turning red. She looks horrible, really horrible, crushed against the kitchen table.

And I can't do anything to help.

I'm so terrified, I can't even move.

I'm just sitting there, watching my dad kill my mum...

It ends. I'm back under the arches with my arms wrapped around his smelly body. I let him go again immediately. My eyes itched with tears I didn't want to have.

It was like I'd been wearing smoked glasses on my brain. I took them off and suddenly I could see what had been happening.

My dad was a liar. Whatever medicine he was taking, I was sure he shouldn't take it and drink alcohol as well. It's not like vodka or whisky were going to help whatever condition he had, now, was it? If he even had a condition. Suddenly, I realised he *didn't* have a condition. He'd spent the money I gave him on booze.

And he hadn't eaten any of the food I'd bought him...

I thought I'd been going to do the right thing, giving him the money I'd saved for Mum's Christmas present. But my brain was working properly now, and I knew it was the wrong thing, entirely the wrong thing. That even being here was the wrong thing. That Andy had been right. That Dill had been right. That even Poppa Burke had been right.

I should have forgotten about my dad.

I should have stayed at home.

I shouldn't have been there at all.

I could feel my heart beating against my ribcage. My mouth went dry.

Dad smiled at me. He said, 'You're a good boy, Jack.'

But it didn't mean anything to me any more. I tried to hide this with a smile. I said, 'How are you feeling?'

I don't know what he said back. I can't remember. It was then I looked around. The circle of men had tightened up a bit around me.

'Do you have the money?'

It wasn't Dad who had spoken to me. It was Dave.

I didn't say anything, so he said it louder. 'Do you have the money?'

I backed away, right into one of the younger men. Dave kind of nodded at him, and the guy grabbed me by the back of my jacket collar with one hand. With the other hand, he went through my pockets until he found the Christmas money. When he let me go, I nearly fell over.

Dave took the money and counted it. He looked at my dad and said, 'You've done well tonight, John.' It was sick to watch my dad cringe and smile, like he was a badly treated dog and Dave was his master.

I said, 'That's for my mum. I want it back.'

But Dave just smiled. He pulled me into the light of the fire and looked at my face one way and then the other. He said, 'Not bad. Not great. But not bad. No wonder the Countess wants him.'

He nodded at one of the other men and said, 'Ring the Countess. Ask him how he wants his package delivered.' When he said the word, 'package', he pointed to me. The other man pulled a mobile out of his pocket. It had to be stolen. Whether it was or not, it was working. He turned his back to speak, making a little gap in the circle.

I ran for it.

I got about three feet before the guy who had rifled my pockets grabbed me again and dragged me back.

I looked at my dad. He couldn't meet my eyes. I said, 'Don't let him do this, Dad.'

I'll never forget what he said.

Dad said, 'It's about time you learned how the world works, Jack. I owe him.'

His voice was as cold as the North Sea. As hard as iron. His piggy eyes squinted at me and he shrugged his shoulders, as if to say it wasn't *his* fault. And I remembered that, too. He used to always shrug his shoulders that way. When he finally let me and Mum out of the kitchen, after four days of terror, he'd shrugged his shoulders that exact same way.

The man finished his phone call and said to Dave, 'He'll be right down. He wants to know if the merchandise is fresh.'

Dave said, 'So far. But I'm sure the Countess can fix that.'

They all looked at me and they all kind of smiled – horrible, creepy, nasty smiles.

It would have been a bad enough smile on *one* face. Replicated nine or ten times on nine or ten faces, it was the most frightening thing I'd ever seen.

Especially since one of the faces was my dad's.

They were going to sell me to the Countess. And my own father didn't seem to mind at all. In fact, he found it a bit funny.

I found out later that Andy had been feeling really uncomfortable all night long. That Tarka couldn't settle on her blanket, that he wasn't selling very many papers... that everything seemed to be going wrong for him. He said he had a nagging feeling that I'd gone down to the arches and even though he tried to tell himself that I was nothing to do with him, that I wasn't his responsibility, he still couldn't stop thinking about it. So he packed up an hour and a half early and left his gear and his money with Otis to come down to the arches and make sure I hadn't gone on my own.

But I didn't know any of that then.

I just knew right then, at like the worst moment of my entire life, Andy and Tarka appeared. Just like angels or something, out of the night.

Everybody turned to look.

Andy just stood there for a moment. And then he said, 'Dave,' in that flat voice he used with him.

And Dave said, 'Andy,' in the same voice.

Andy walked closer and the circle widened to let him in. Then it closed behind him. He looked at me for the first time then. I was so glad to see him, I nearly started to cry.

Andy said, 'Tarka, go to Jack.' And she did. She licked my fingers once and then sat right by my left foot. The guy who kept grabbing me moved away a little and Andy smiled.

He said to me, 'I want you to take Tarka back to the bridge. Now.'

I didn't even think about not doing it. I took her

lead and started to walk out of the circle. The guy who'd grabbed me before grabbed me again. Tarka made this rumbling noise in her throat, not quite a growl, more like a promise of trouble. The guy dropped my arm like it was radioactive. Tarka and I walked out of the circle.

And then I looked back. All the men were picking up pieces of timber. They weren't fuel. They were weapons. One man gave a stick to Dave and he walked up to Andy and just whacked him, hard as he could, on the side of the head. Andy fell to the ground, rolling over and covering his head with his arms. He saw me standing there with Tarka and screamed, 'Go, Jack! Run!'

There was nothing else I could do. I ran.

For about twenty yards.

When I ran right into a uniform.

9.

Respect

You see, another thing I didn't know was that when Andy found Dill waiting for me on the bridge, he'd asked him to ring the police. He said to tell the police that Andy Powers said there was trouble at the arches. What Andy didn't know is that Dill doesn't have a mobile, either. Dill's Dad doesn't allow them.

So Dill had been banging on doors and ringing bells, trying to get the posh people in the cobbled terrace to let him use a telephone, but nobody had let him in. In fact, somebody had called the cops and told them there was a black kid running wild in their street.

So Dill got the police all right. He got arrested. Still, Dill's not going to be our marketing manager for nothing. He told them exactly what was going on, and with his charm and gift of the gab, they immediately called their controller and started down the path.

Which is when I ran head first into one of the constable's stomachs and nearly winded him.

I said, 'You've got to help Andy! They're killing him!'

They left me with Tarka and took off running down the path. One of them called for an ambulance while he ran, talking on his little shoulder radio/phone thing. I know this, because I was right behind them. I didn't know what I could do for Andy. I'd been pretty useless so far. But Tarka and I both wanted to be there. And even if *I* hadn't, I'm pretty sure she would have dragged me back on her own.

The less normal ones let out a roar when they saw the police running by, which must have been a warning of some kind. By the time we got to the wall and the fire barrel, Dave, my dad, and all their friends were gone. Tarka ran to something lying on the ground, which turned out to be Andy. She whined and licked his face.

The police turned him over on his side. One of them stroked back his hair.

Andy was bleeding in so many places – from his head and from his nose. He had a cut on his arm, as well, that went right through his two jumpers. One of his legs was at a funny angle which meant, I knew, that it was broken.

The one who had stroked back Andy's hair took a handkerchief from his pocket and held it to the head wound. The other one turned to me. He said, 'Did you see who did this?'

And I didn't think any nonsense about not being a grass at all. I said, 'A man named John Burke and a man called Dave. There were other men, too.'

The policeman seeing to Andy looked like he was going to cry. He said, 'Oh, hell.'

When the one standing by me said, 'What?', the first policeman explained.

'Dave,' he said. 'It's Dave Powers. Andy's dad.'

I just couldn't believe it. Dave was Andy's father? I remembered the way he spoke to him in that flat voice, and worse, the way Dave had just whacked Andy in the head with the timber, as if Andy was just a *thing*, an obstacle, something in his way.

No, I couldn't believe anyone could do that to their own flesh and blood.

But then I thought about my dad. The way he'd smiled when they talked about me as 'merchandise'. And then I *could* believe it.

I just didn't want to.

The policeman by me said, 'Don't worry. We'll get them. They're going to pay for this.'

Tarka kept running to Andy and back to me. She was so worried.

So was I. I found Andy's mad little hat in the mud. It was ripped. There must have been nails in those pieces of timber they'd used on him.

The ambulance men arrived and they had a board-like thing. They put this big collar around Andy's head and neck. He moaned a little. It seemed to take them forever to get him loaded on to the board thing. Then the four of them carried him to the ambulance. The nice constable got in and Tarka jumped in after him. I still had the other end of her lead. I looked at the constable and the ambulance man in the back and they looked at each other. Then the policeman said, 'You might as well come, too.'

His partner said he'd take Dill home and meet us at the hospital to get a full statement. He asked for my name and phone number and said he'd try to get hold of my parents, but that he'd have to call the child protection officers if he couldn't. I kept nodding, but I didn't really take it in. I was watching the ambulance man try and stop Andy's head from bleeding.

I'd always wanted to ride in an emergency vehicle, you know, blue lights flashing, sirens blaring. I thought it would be really exciting. But when you're watching someone you care about hurting, you don't really register it. You just don't care about anything else but whether or not they're going to make it.

I said, 'Is he going to be OK?'

And the ambulance guy said, 'I'm not sure, son. He took a few knocks tonight.'

The nice constable met my eyes and I could see he was just as upset as I was. Nobody said anything else, all that long ride.

I put my arms around Tarka and she whined, licking behind my ears. For some reason, that's the thing, out of everything else that had happened, that made me start to cry.

The lights of A&E seemed really bright when the doors opened. Tarka and I sat still while everyone else got Andy out and on to a rolling bed thing. They ran with him into a room, leaving me and the constable behind. I had to tie Tarka outside because they wouldn't let her in. She settled right down on the pavement, good as gold, like she knew we had to wait.

'She's been here before,' the constable said. When we went inside, he moved into a corner and started speaking on his shoulder phone.

Somebody, it might have been a nurse, came and asked me a load of questions. I really couldn't answer that many of them. I didn't know how old Andy was or where he lived. I told her he sold the *Big Issue* and she said she could find out all the rest by calling their office. She gave me a big polystyrene cup full of cocoa and told me I'd done well. Then she showed me down the hall, out of A&E to the waiting room. She said someone would come and tell me soon how Andy was doing. She said the constable would join me in a moment.

I felt cold and everything seemed grey. Every time I had a sip of the cocoa, I felt better (probably because it raised my blood sugar level), but the effect didn't seem to last long. It took me about ten sips to even get down to the waiting room door and another two to open it.

And then I saw her.

It was Mum. She was sitting on one of the rows of chairs. Her light brown hair was down over the neck of that oatmeal-coloured jumper that she liked to wear with her jeans. She'd been chewing her lip and half her lipstick had come off, but she still looked beautiful.

She was as surprised to see me as I was to see her, her big green eyes got all wide. She said, 'Jack, *darling*, what's happened?'

I ran right into her arms. I could feel her kiss the top of my head. She was so warm and soft. I just wanted to stay there forever.

Richard was there, too.

When I finally let go of my mum, he pulled me on to his lap. He took the cup out of my hand and prised Andy's muddy hat from my fingers. 'What's going on?' he asked me. 'Did something happen on the Scout trip?'

I shook my head. 'No,' I said. And then I thought for a moment. I said, 'Why are *you* here?'

My mum cleared her throat for a second. 'It's Poppa Burke,' she said. 'He's dying.'

We all sort of looked at each other, if you know what I mean, kind of getting about a million questions and answers lined up in our heads. But then the door opened and the lady who had been so nice to me was back. She said, 'Andy's going to be all right.'

I said, 'But what about his leg?'

'Oh, that's broken,' she said, 'But it's a simple fracture. He's not going to be running any marathons for a while, but it will be OK. The head wound was mainly superficial. He has a little bit of a concussion, but again, not that bad. He'll look terrible for a week or two – he's going to have two really black eyes and his jaw is broken – but he should be fine. His arm was cut pretty deep, but it just missed the artery. That will be sore, too. I think he'll probably be our guest for a week or two.'

I started to cry again, this time from relief. I managed to say, 'Thanks for telling me.'

She patted my shoulder. She said, 'Are these your parents?' And when I nodded she told me, 'The policeman is on his way. He's going to want to ask you some questions, if you're up to it.'

I nodded again. I said, 'I'm up to it.'

But my mum said, '*Police*!' She looked at me and then at Richard. 'What's going on? Who is Andy?' she asked. 'Are you in trouble?'

The nice constable opened the door. He said

to her, 'No. Jack's not in trouble. Jack's a brave lad. You should be proud of him.'

In a way, it was good that they were all there, so I only had to tell the whole thing once. But in a way, it wasn't, because it took forever to tell. Somebody was always interrupting me. My mum just couldn't understand how easy it had been for me to leave the house.

When I finished, Richard asked me if Tarka was still outside. When I said yes, he said, 'I'm just going to make sure she's all right. Get her some water.' He lifted me off his lap and put me on another chair. But then he came back for a second and cuddled me hard before he left the room.

That's when I told Mum and the police about the letters. My mum shook her head at me. Her big green eyes were full of tears. She said, 'Those letters are from years ago, Jack. Before you were born. When your dad was at university. He used to write to me every day. I was crying because I had loved him so much... before...'

The second policeman asked, 'Was John

Burke ever violent with you, Mrs Burke?'

And my mother nodded sadly. She said, 'It was when he started hurting Jack that I knew things had to change. I put John's clothes out and changed the locks on the doors. And then Jack and I went away on holiday for two weeks. Cornwall. My parents paid for it.'

And I remembered...

My mother's face has faded to a light green bruise. I can only see it because the sun is so bright. It's winter, but the sun is shining in that hard, white way it does that time of year.

The waves are crashing on to the shore, so loud that my mum has to shout three times before I hear what she's asking me.

'...hungry?' is all I hear.

I nod and she takes my hand. She starts pulling me up the long cliff path. Halfway there, we stop and sit on a big rock together. You can see forever. The sea stretches to the sky impossibly far away. It's cold, even in the sun. I lean back into my mum and she wraps her arms around me.

For the first time I feel safe again, and I start to cry.

Mum doesn't say anything. She just holds me like that while I shake and sob. It lasts a long time.

Then she passes a little plastic pocket of tissues over my shoulder. I wipe up my face and blow my nose and then pass them back, shoving the dirty ones in my jacket pocket.

She pulls me to my feet and hugs me again.

And then we start to walk...

I'd forgotten all about that trip to Cornwall. I'd forgotten all about a lot of things.

My mum had been talking. She finished saying, '...and we never heard from him again.'

'But you never talked to Jack about the things his dad had done.' The first policeman looked at her. His eyes weren't warm or cold. They just watched her.

She swallowed, her throat moving so much that you could see it through the neck of her jumper. 'No,' she said. 'I thought he'd forgotten. And I didn't think it was right. I didn't think it was fair for Jack just to hear my side of it and never hear his father's side. So I never said anything about the drink... or the violence.' She looked at me and said, 'I'm sorry about that now.'

My mum slid down off her chair and knelt down on the lino in front of me. She said, 'You could have been hurt, really hurt. And it would have been my fault for never talking to you about John, about what he was really like.'

I said, 'I gave him your Christmas money.'

'What?' She looked at me with her forehead all wrinkled up. 'What Christmas money?'

'I'd been saving up. All year. I had over seventy quid. I was going to buy you something really nice. But I gave it to Dad. He said he needed it. And even when I knew he was lying, they took it anyway.'

We looked at each other again. It was strange how you can live with someone and not know all that much about them, about what goes on inside them. In a way, it was like I'd never really seen my mum before, not properly. And she said later that she felt the same way about me. It was only a second, but it seemed to last a long, long time.

Finally, she said, 'I'm really sorry, Jack.'

And this time, *I* cried.

My mum smiled at me, and it was like the whole place disappeared – the hospital, the police, everything. It was like a whole universe with just us inside. And she said, 'Oh, Jack. I love you so.' She gave me another massive cuddle, in front of everyone, and I didn't care at all.

My stomach rumbled. I was hungry again.

10.

Do Right Woman, Do Right Man

Poppa Burke was in intensive care, which is right by A&E. I wasn't allowed to go into that ward, but I could see him through the window. There were four or five people in there, and they were all so sick you couldn't tell which ones were men and which ones were women. I could barely recognise Poppa Burke. I mainly knew who he was because Nana Burke was standing by his bed.

Richard stood with me while Mum went in. I could see Mum take Nana Burke's hand. Nana Burke leaned against my mum and my mum put her arm around Nana Burke. Richard put his hand on my shoulder. He asked, 'Are you OK with all this stuff, Jack?'

I nodded. I didn't have that remote, slow feeling I'd had before I drank the cocoa. It was all kind of horrible, but it was different. I didn't feel like I couldn't handle it or anything.

Richard put his arm around me, and I kind of leaned into him, just like Nana Burke had done with Mum. Richard said, 'I'm really sorry your dad let you down, Jack.'

I said, 'You knew he would. You tried to tell me.'

But he said, 'Well, for once I wish I had been wrong.' He cuddled me closer and I put my arm around his back. We stood that way for a long time, watching Poppa Burke die.

A while afterwards, I woke up in the waiting room. Richard was shaking me. I sat up. Mum and Nana Burke were standing there and my mum said, 'He's gone.'

My eyes filled with tears.

'You see?' Nana Burke said to my mum. 'Even

Jack can cry for him. Why can't I?'

She sat down, wringing her dry hankie as if it was the hankie's fault.

My mum said, 'Mollie, what you had together was...' she searched for the right word and found it, '...complicated. I don't think you can expect your emotions to be simple, when your relationship was so complicated.'

Nana Burke made a snorting sound. 'Complicated,' she echoed. 'That's one way of putting it.' She looked at my mum and me and said, 'You did the right thing, Laura, when you put my son out on the street. I'm sorry I ever gave you grief about it.'

Mum sighed. She said, 'I don't know what's right or wrong, Mollie. Maybe you did the right thing sticking by your husband all those years.'

Nana Burke made the snorting sound again. She said, 'Five broken jaws. Left arm broken twice, right arm three times. I lost count of the ribs. He dislocated my shoulders over and over. He had this phase where he used to like to swing me around the lounge by my arm before he let me fly into the furniture...' her voice caught in her throat and then, at last, the tears started to come. 'It was the drink,' she choked. 'He was a good man, really. It was just when he drank...' Now she couldn't speak any more for crying.

That's what had happened to my grandmother's face. My grandfather had beaten it out of shape. When I realised that, it made me feel sick. I think I would have thrown up, if there had been anything in my stomach *to* throw up.

I went to her and put my arms around her and she cried into the jumper that she'd knitted for me herself. I looked over her head at my mum. She was leaning against Richard and tears were rolling down her pretty face.

I was suddenly, fiercely, glad my mum had thrown my dad out of the house, before he had made her face lopsided. I was glad my mother was so pretty still.

The last bit of my hate for her evaporated away while Nana Burke cried.

Nana Burke cried for a long time. Finally, she stopped. She was holding my hand. Somehow, although I didn't remember it, I had found Andy's mad little hat before I'd gone to sleep and I was holding it in my other hand. She took it from me and looked at the mud on it, putting her finger in the hole and making a clucking sound. She wiped her eyes with her hankie one last time and said, 'Do you want me to make you another one of these?'

It was really Sunday morning by the time Nana Burke had finished signing things. The sun was out. The ground was white with frost. Richard suggested we all go out to breakfast. He knew this caff, he said, and we could all do with a good fry-up. It sounded like such a great idea I didn't even say anything about fat content or empty calories.

Before we went, though, we peeped into Andy's room. He was awake.

I introduced everybody and he waved. He couldn't talk, but they'd given him a pad and a pencil.

The first thing he wrote was, 'Tarka?'

Richard said, 'She's fine. She's outside, but she's

under cover and she's had something to drink.'

Andy kind of grinned, as much as he could grin. He looked really terrible. His face was all shiny and you could tell that it was going to have some bad bruising by tea-time. They'd had to shave part of his hair off to stitch up his head. He had a tube in his arm and his leg was in plaster. He wrote again. 'Where will she stay?'

Only he'd left out the 'h' in 'where'. His handwriting was awful, too. It looked like something a four-year-old would do.

But we were all more worried about what it said than how he'd said it.

I looked at Mum, but she said, 'I'm sure we'll figure something out. Problem is, Richard and I are both at work all day.'

Nana Burke said, 'I'm not.'

We all turned to look at her, and she said it again. She said, 'I'm not gone all day. I can look after the doggie.'

Andy grinned again. He wrote, 'THANK YOU' in great big scrawly letters.

Nana Burke walked to the bedside and patted

his good arm. 'I'll come and see you tomorrow, too,' she said. 'Do you want anything? I always get the paper at home. I'll bring that.'

Andy gave a little sigh and his head fell back on to the pillow as if he was tired.

'I'll see you tomorrow,' Nana Burke promised.

'And we'll see you tomorrow night,' Richard said. We all turned to go, but my mum turned back.

She said, 'Thank you, Andy,' really softly, stroking his hair back out of his eyes, just like the policeman had done.

Andy closed his bruised eyes.

We left down another hallway. And there was Otis, sitting on a chair. He stood as we came up to him. 'He gonna be OK, Jack?' he asked me. 'They wouldn't let me in with the gear, and I couldn't leave it. I been worried.'

I told him what the nurse had said the night before and Otis sucked his teeth. He said, 'That Dave is bad news, man. I told Andy to stay away from his dad.'

I said, 'It was my fault, Otis.'

But Otis said, 'Shoo,' and shook his head. He said, 'Ain't nobody can make Andy Powers do what he don't wanna do. And ain't nobody can stop him when he decides to do something. It ain't your fault, little man.'

Which made me feel a bit better.

Richard said, 'Andy's sleeping. We're just going out for some breakfast, Otis. Do you want to come along?'

Otis motioned to the side of the chair where all his things were still on his trolley. Andy's bag was sitting on top, with Tarka's blanket rolled up on top of that. He said, 'That's nice of you, but I got all this stuff.'

Richard shrugged. He said, 'My boot's empty.'

Otis grinned. He said, 'Sure. I'd like that.'

So we all went out to breakfast, including Tarka, who ate *five* sausages. Even *I* only ate three. We dropped Otis off at his B&B, Tarka and Nana Burke off at her house and then went back to our place.

Mum poured me a bath with essential oils in it and then I ate some more. About five o'clock

I went to bed. I slept for twenty-two hours. I've read that you can't really catch up on your sleep, that you have to just sleep regularly your eight or nine hours every night to feel rested. But I think the sleep experts might have that one wrong. Maybe Dill and I can look into it sometime.

When I woke up, I had to run to the bathroom. Nobody had told my waterworks I was asleep. They were wide awake and just about to work.

I came back to my room and my mum was there, smoothing out my sheets. I went to her and again she gave me a huge cuddle. I leaned into her, smelling how clean she always smelled. We spent a while like that.

Then she said, 'Back to bed for one more night. You can get up tomorrow.'

I still felt tired, too tired to argue. I climbed into bed. But I said, 'Can I watch your little telly?'

She sat down on the edge of the bed and smiled. 'Maybe, but I think you'll be too busy for television.'

'What do you mean?'

'I have four worried children in my living room. Dill Hanson's been there all day. Anne came after school. Scott and Wesley came together. Scott's mum is in our kitchen, making sandwiches, right now. She brought over all kinds of snacks.'

'What? Why?'

Mum shrugged. 'They felt responsible, especially Dill, for letting you do all this. Dill's mum and dad more or less told him that if anything had happened to you, it would have been Dill's fault for not telling anyone what you were up to.'

'But that's crazy!'

Mum shrugged again. 'Anne's parents told her the same thing, when they heard about it. And Scott's mum, Louisa, is downstairs telling them all even now.'

I sat there. My mum was smiling. 'Louisa said that when you care for somebody, you're supposed to do just that – care for them.'

My eyes filled with tears. Anne, Scott, Dill and Wesley. They weren't 'a group' or 'a crowd'. They were my friends. They cared for me.

'The four of them are sitting down there as quiet as mice. They're reading their homework and biting their nails, waiting for you to wake up. Will you see them?'

I started to get out of bed, but my mum pushed me back down. 'I'll send them up,' she said. 'With some sandwiches. If you're hungry?'

I was ravenous. And that was the best I ever felt in my whole life, waiting there, hearing all the footsteps running up the stairs.

Knowing where to end this is almost as hard as telling you the truth.

I talked to my mates at lunch yesterday about it and Anne said that I should make a list of everything that's relevant and not bore anyone with things that don't really concern the story.

In that case, there's not a lot more for me to tell you.

Dill and I took our frog project to our town's annual science competition and got a yellow ribbon for third place. Even though we only got third, we were the ones with our pictures in the paper. Or Dill was, anyway. They cropped most of me out of it. Mum was furious and kept going on about how it wasn't fair, but I didn't really mind. I mean, that's the way the world works, doesn't it? People as good-looking as Dill are always going to have some things easier.

Anne said if it wasn't for Dill's looks, the whole science competition probably wouldn't have made the paper at all. Of course, she didn't say that in front of Dill.

Poppa Burke was buried. He'd planned the whole thing himself, even the songs. There was a lot about forgiveness in them all.

Tons of people came to see him off, but my dad wasn't one of them. Richard said we probably wouldn't see him or Dave for quite a while, since they were wanted by the police for GBH. The nice constable came by and he said the same thing. He also said that they hoped to put the Countess out of business quite soon. I thought about the thin girl, thinking the Countess was her friend. I hoped she was all right when whatever was going to happen, happened.

Andy is living with Nana Burke now. They say it's only until he feels better, but he's been back to work and everything for quite a while, and I reckon they both like the company. They just don't like to say.

Andy's still selling the *Big Issue*. He got so far behind on his computer course that he failed the exam. It gets offered again in the summer and he's going to take it again then. In the meantime, Richard is tutoring him on his language skills and Nana Burke makes him read the paper to her every day while she knits.

She's knitting up a storm these days. When Andy told her how much he paid for his hat, she just couldn't believe it. She talked to a lady at her church and got this stall on the craft market our town does on Fridays. She sells all kinds of things on it – hats, jumpers with hoods, jumpers with big daisies and smiley faces on them – and she takes orders as well. She's making a lot of money and she seems really happy, though sometimes she still cries about Poppa Burke.

Tarka loves Nana Burke's fire and Nana Burke's carpet. Andy has to practically drag her out to work at night, he says. And he complains she's getting fat, so I take her for long walks every Saturday. I'm even going to take her on our next Scout's outing, if the Scoutmaster doesn't mind. Richard's going to ask.

Otis and Andy came to Christmas at our house with Nana Burke and Nana and Poppa Lacey. We found out a lot about Otis that day. He used to live in America and he still has five children who live over there. That's why he never has any money: he sends almost everything he makes to them. He told us that when he was in the big time, he spent all his money on himself, on drinking and good times. He said he gives his kids more money now that he's a homeless busker than when he was a back-up singer for Marvin Gaye on a huge wage packet.

He showed us pictures. Two of his children are

at uni and he has seven grandchildren. Mum made him use our phone to ring them all. Later I saw Poppa Lacey give her money to pay the bill with.

It was strange how we all got along. You looked around the room and you'd think we would all just be strangers to each other. But it wasn't like that.

It still isn't.

Two weeks ago, I got assigned a 'trauma counsellor'. I was supposed to get her right after all of this happened, but evidently they're short-handed. And evidently, I wasn't all that traumatised, compared to some of the people Rasminda works with. This story is the homework I'm doing for her. I'm working on keeping all my memories, even when something happens I don't like.

Sometimes, I wake up screaming and sweating, with memories of my dad. But it's not anything that happened recently, it's all the old stuff. Those four days in the kitchen come back to me over and over.

Rasminda says it's all part of the process and that I shouldn't worry too much about it. So I don't, much. I even went to an overnight at Scott's place with Wesley and Dill. They were betting on whether or not I'd have a nightmare there. Dill said I wouldn't. He won three pounds and one of the pounds was mine.

Richard and my mum are planning their wedding. They say it's going to be a simple affair, but it looks pretty complicated to me. The kitchen table is buried under all kinds of paperwork and magazines, and Mum is always asking me about which colour of peach I think is nicest or if three-ply serviettes are really that much better than two-ply. Like I can tell the difference!

When it gets bad, Richard says he's got a load of marking and I say I've got a load of homework. He goes back to his place and I hide in my room.

But sometimes I go back to his place with him. We listen to soul music and try and cook things from this excellent Chinese cookbook Richard found at a car boot sale. Sometimes, Richard lets me stay up late and we go down and listen to Otis for a while. Sometimes, he drops me home after, but other times I spend the night on his sofa.

I nearly always wake up screaming at Richard's. He comes and sits with me until I get back to sleep. If it's been really bad, sometimes we play a game, sitting there in our pyjamas at two or something in the morning, like a little break. It almost makes it worth it.

The whole wedding thing can get to be complete madness. Richard says we men just need to leave her to it. So we do. Quite a lot, actually.

Mum doesn't seem to mind at all.

Sometimes I turn around and look at her, as Richard and I go out of the door together, just to see if it makes her sad or angry or anything to be left behind on her own.

But she always seems to be smiling.